EMMA

JANE AUSTEN

Simplified
and brought within the 1,800 word vocabulary
of the New Method Supplementary Readers Stage 5
by

Michael West
and
E. P. Hart

Illustrated by Will Nickless

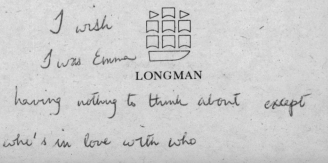

I wish
I was Emma

LONGMAN

having nothing to think about except

who's in love with who

LONGMAN GROUP LIMITED
London

*Associated companies, branches and representatives
throughout the world*

First published in this edition 1956
Fourth impression 1960
*New impressions * 1962 (twice); * 1963; * 1964 (twice);*
** 1965; * 1966; * 1967; * 1970; * 1971 (twice);*
** 1974; * 1975;*
* 1977

ISBN 0 582 53510 7

*Printed in Hong Kong by
Dai Nippon Printing Co (H.K.) Ltd*

CONTENTS

Contents

LIST OF PERSONS IN THE BOOK

Mr Woodhouse—a rich man who is very afraid of catching cold.

Emma—his daughter, aged 20.

Mr George Knightley—a friend of Mr Woodhouse; he "seldom praises Emma."

Mr John Knightley—brother of Mr George Knightley; married Emma's sister, *Isabella*.

Miss Taylor—Emma's governess, now married to *Mr Weston*.

Frank Weston Churchill—Mr Weston's son by a former marriage.

Mr Elton—young, unmarried. Emma wished him to marry Harriet.

Harriet Smith—Her father and mother are not known. She lives at *Mrs Goddard's* school. She is pretty, but not very clever.

Mr Martin—a farmer wishing to marry Harriet Smith.

Miss Bates—a kind lady who talks too much.

Jane Fairfax—her niece.

Mrs Elton—formerly Miss Hawkins; a rich woman who marries Mr Elton.

Mr and Mrs Cole—business people who are rising in the world.

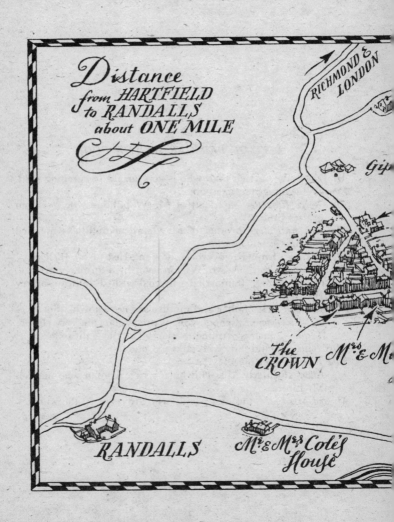

Distance *from* HARTFIELD *to* RANDALLS *about* ONE MILE

RICHMOND & LONDON

Gip

The CROWN

Mrs & Mr

RANDALLS

Mr & Mrs Cole's House

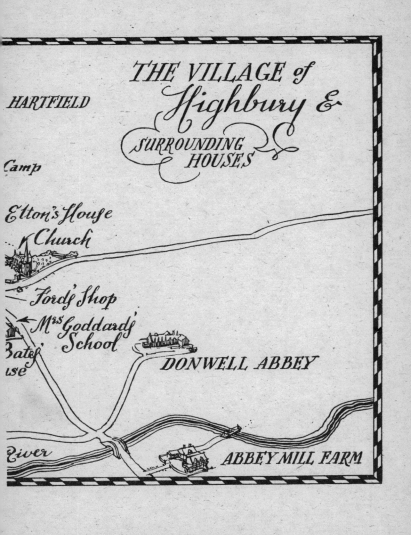

THE VILLAGE of
Highbury &
SURROUNDING HOUSES

HARTFIELD

Camp

Elton's House

Church

Ford's Shop

Mrs Goddard's School

Bates' House

DONWELL ABBEY

River

ABBEY MILL FARM

One

"POOR MISS TAYLOR!"

Emma Woodhouse was beautiful, clever and rich, and had lived to be twenty years old with very little to pain or trouble her. Her father, a rich country gentleman, loved her and spoiled her. Her mother died long ago, and Emma was taught at home by an excellent governess, Miss Taylor. When Emma grew up Miss Taylor still lived in the house, less as a governess than as a friend. This arrangement had gone on for a long time: then Miss Taylor married Mr. Weston, a gentleman who lived in the same village of Highbury. It was a large village, almost a small town.

Miss Taylor—now Mrs. Weston—would not be far away, and Emma would see her often, yet she felt sorrow for the loss of her friend. Her father also disliked change of any kind, and he was very sorry to part with Miss Taylor.

It was the evening after Miss Taylor's marriage: Emma and her father sat at their evening meal.

"Poor Miss Taylor," said Mr. Woodhouse. "I wish she were here again. What a pity that Mr. Weston ever thought of her!"

Emma smiled and talked as cheerfully as she could so as to keep her father from sad thoughts; but, when dinner was ended and they sat by the fire, "Poor Miss Taylor," he said again. "She has done a sad thing for herself. She would have been a great deal happier if she had spent all the rest of her life here with us at Hartfield*."

"I cannot agree with you, father," said Emma; "you know that I cannot. Mr. Weston is a pleasant, excellent man, and he deserves a good wife; and you would not have wanted Miss Taylor to live with us and bear all my fanciful manners, when she might have a house of her own."

* Hartfield is the name of Mr. Woodhouse's house.

"A house of her own!" said Mr. Woodhouse. "What is the good of a house of her own? This house is three times as large as hers—and you are never fanciful, my dear."

Emma replied, "We shall often be going to see them, and they will be coming to see us! We shall always be meeting. We must go and pay our marriage visit very soon."

JAMES, THE COACHMAN

"My dear," said her father, "how am I to get so far? Mr. Weston's house, Randalls, is such a distance. I could not walk half so far."

"No, father; nobody thought of your walking. We must go in the carriage."

"The carriage! But James will not like us to use the horses for such a little way; and where are the poor horses to be while we are paying our visit?"

"They are to be put with Mr. Weston's horses," said Emma. "You know, father, that we talked it all over with Mr. Weston last night."

Two

MR. GEORGE KNIGHTLEY

At this moment a visitor arrived. This was Mr. George Knightley, an old friend of the family. He was closely united with it because his brother John had married Emma's elder sister Isabella. Mr. Knightley lived about a mile away and he often came to visit Emma and her father.

Mr. Woodhouse asked many questions about "poor Isabella" and her children. When these questions had been answered he said: "It is very kind of you, Mr. Knightley, to come out so late in the day to see us. I am afraid you must have had a difficult walk."

"Not at all, sir," said Mr. Knightley. "It is a beautiful moonlight night, and so warm that I must draw back from your great fire."

"But you must have found it very wet and dirty. I hope you will not catch cold."

"Dirty, sir! Look at my shoes. Not a spot on them."

"Well, that is a surprise. We have had a lot of rain here. I wanted them to put off the marriage because of the rain. Poor Miss Taylor! That is a sad business."

"You may say poor Mr. and Miss Woodhouse, if you wish," said Mr. Knightley; "but I cannot possibly say 'poor Miss Taylor'. Surely it is fortunate for her that she is married— and to so good a man as Mr. Weston. It must be better to have only one to please instead of two."

"I MUST DRAW BACK FROM THE FIRE"

"Especially when *one* of those two is such a fanciful, trouble-some creature," said Emma, playfully. "That is what you have in your head, I know, Mr. Knightley. That is what you would say if my father were not here."

"I believe it is very true, my dear," said Mr. Woodhouse. "I am afraid I am sometimes very fanciful and troublesome."

"My dearest father," said Emma, "you do not think I could mean *you*. What an idea! Oh no! I meant only myself. Mr. Knightley loves to find fault with me, you know—in a joke—it is all a joke. We always say what we like to one another."

"Emma knows that I seldom praise her," said Mr. Knightley, "but I did not mean to speak unkindly of anybody. Miss Taylor has been used to having two persons to please. She will now have only one."

Three

HARRIET

Mr. Woodhouse liked to have his friends come and see him, especially now that "poor Miss Taylor" no longer lived in the house. She and her husband and Mr. Knightley often came. Another visitor was Mr. Elton, a young gentleman who lived alone. He was as yet unmarried, and he was always glad to come and see Mr. Woodhouse and his lovely daughter. Others who came were Mrs. and Miss Bates and Mrs. Goddard.

Mrs. Goddard kept a school for young ladies. One day, when she was coming to Hartfield, she said to Emma, "Would you mind, Miss Woodhouse, if I bring with me one of my pupils, Miss Harriet Smith?"

"My father and I will be very pleased to see Miss Smith," said Emma. "I know her very well by sight and have long felt an interest in her because of her beauty."

Harriet Smith was the "natural" daughter of some person not married to the mother. Somebody had placed her, several years ago, at Mrs. Goddard's school. This was all that was known of her history. She was a very pretty girl. She was short and fair, with blue eyes and a look of great sweetness. Before the evening was over Emma was as much pleased with her manners as with her beauty. She made up her mind to become a friend to Harriet. She thought that the friends whom Harriet had at present were not worthy of her.

Harriet had been staying with a family of the name of Martin who rented* a large farm from Mr. Knightley. Emma knew that Mr. Knightley thought well of them, but she felt that they could not have good manners, or be suitable friends for such a girl as she hoped Harriet would become. She decided to separate Harriet from these honest but simple friends, and to bring her into good company. In this way she would form Harriet's opinions and her manners.

Four

ABBEY-MILL FARM

Emma was quick and decided in her ways and she lost no time in making friends with Harriet. "I shall love Harriet as someone to whom I can be useful," she said to herself.

Her first attempts at usefulness led her to try to find out who were Harriet's father and mother. Harriet could not tell her, but she talked freely about Mrs. Goddard and the teachers and the girls; and much about her friends, the Martins of Abbey-Mill Farm.

"I spent two months with them, and I was oh! so happy. They have *two* sitting-rooms! One of the rooms is quite as large as Mrs. Goddard's room. And they have a servant, and eight cows, and a wooden house in the garden where they sit and have tea in the summer."

Harriet also told about Mr. Martin: "Mr. Martin is so kind, so helpful," she said. "He went three miles one day to bring me some nuts† because I said that I loved eating nuts. His mother and sisters love him very much."

***

* To rent = to pay money for the use of land or houses.
† Nut.—the seed of a tree, contained in a hard shell.

"He is not married, then?" said Emma. Harriet said that Mr. Martin was not married. Mrs. Martin said that he was a very good son and that when he married he would be a good husband. But there was no hurry for him to marry.

"Well done, Mrs. Martin!" thought Emma. "You know what you are doing!"

Emma then asked: "Is Mr. Martin a good-looking man?"

"Oh! No; not good-looking. I thought him rather ugly at first, but I do not think so now. But have you never seen him? He is in Highbury every week and he has passed you very often."

"That may be, and I may have seen him fifty times without having any idea of his name. Do you know how old he is?"

"He was twenty-four on the eighth of last June, and my birthday is the twenty-third; just fifteen days difference."

"Only twenty-four! That is too young to marry. His mother is perfectly right not to be in a hurry. Six years from now, if he could meet a good sort of young woman in the same rank as his own, with a little money, it might be very desirable."

"Six years! Dear Miss Woodhouse, he would be thirty years old."

"Well," said Emma, "a man must be earning enough money when he marries. Most men of his class are not able to earn enough for marriage until they are thirty."

Five

MR. MARTIN

One day, when Emma and Harriet were walking together in Highbury, they met Mr. Martin. He looked very respectfully at Emma and with great satisfaction at her companion. Emma was not sorry to see Mr. Martin and to form an opinion of him. She walked on a little while he and Harriet talked. When he had gone, Harriet came to Emma and said, "Well, Miss Woodhouse, is he like what you expected?"

"He is certainly not very good looking," said Emma, "but that is not so important as the fact that he is clearly not a gentleman. I had no right to expect much, and I did not expect much; but I had no idea that he would be so without manners."

"To be sure," said Harriet in a sad voice, "he is not like gentlemen."

"I think," said Emma, "that, since you have known us, you have often been in the company of gentlemen, such as Mr. Weston and Mr. Elton. Compare Mr. Martin with either of *them*. You must see the difference."

"Oh yes, there is a great difference. But Mr. Weston is almost an old man. He must be between forty and fifty."

"Then what do you say to Mr. Elton? He is about the same age as Mr. Martin, but what a difference there is in their manners! Mr. Elton is pleasant, graceful and gentle. He seems to me to have grown very gentle of late. I do not know whether he wishes particularly to please either of us, but it seems to me that his manners are softer than they used to be. If he means anything, it must be to please you."

Emma then repeated some warm praise of Harriet which she had drawn from Mr. Elton.

Harriet blushed and smiled, and said that she had always thought Mr. Elton very pleasant.

Mr. Elton was the person fixed on by Emma for driving the young farmer out of Harriet's head.

Six

THE PICTURE

Mr. Elton was often at Hartfield, and Emma was glad to find that he approved of what she had done for Harriet Smith.

"You have given her all that she needed," he said. "She was beautiful when she came to you, but you have made her graceful and easy."

"I am glad you think I have been useful to her," said Emma; "she only wanted drawing out. She has naturally a sweet temper: I have done very little."

"You have done much—very much," said Mr. Elton, looking eagerly at Emma.

HARRIET SITS FOR HER PICTURE

Emma was well satisfied with the interest he showed in her friend.

On another day, when Mr. Elton was at Hartfield, an idea came suddenly to Emma.

"Harriet," she said, "did you ever sit for your picture?"

Harriet was just going out of the room, but she turned and said, "Oh, dear, no—never."

When she went out Emma said, "How beautiful a good picture of her would be. I may perhaps attempt it myself."

"Please do so, Miss Woodhouse," said Mr. Elton. "It will indeed be a delight. I know how good your drawings are."

"Well," said Emma, "if you wish it so much I think I *shall* attempt it."

Harriet came back, and she was soon asked to sit for her picture. The sitting began at once. When Emma began to draw, Mr. Elton stood behind her, watching her as she worked.

"No doubt," Emma thought, "he stands behind me so that he may be able to look at Harriet without being rude."

The sitting was very satisfactory. Emma was well enough pleased with her first day's work to wish to go on. Harriet was to sit again the next day; and Mr. Elton—just as he ought— asked if he might come to watch how the work went on.

"Certainly!" said Emma, "we shall be most happy to consider you as one of the party."

When the picture was finished Mr. Woodhouse came to see it.

"It is very pretty," he said, "just as your pictures always are, my dear. The only thing I do not like is that she seems to be sitting out of doors. It makes one think that she must catch cold."

"But my dear father, it is supposed to be summer. Look at the tree."

"But it is never safe to sit out of doors, my dear."

"You, sir, may say anything," said Mr. Elton, "but I think it is a most happy thought to place Miss Smith out of doors. Any other place would have been much less in character. I never saw such a good picture. I cannot keep my eyes from it."

The next thing wanted was to get the picture framed. Mr. Elton at once offered to take it to London and choose the frame according to Emma's wishes.

"What a precious packet!" he said with a tender sigh, as he received it.

"This man is certainly very much in love," thought Emma. "He is an excellent young man, and will suit Harriet exactly."

Seven

AN OFFER OF MARRIAGE

On the day on which Mr. Elton went to London, Harriet came to Hartfield as usual after breakfast. She came with an excited look, as if something extraordinary had happened.

"Oh! Miss Woodhouse," she said, "what *do* you think! Mr. Martin came to Mrs. Goddard's this morning with a packet for one of his sisters, and when he was gone, and the packet was opened, it contained a letter for me. And what do you think it was?——An offer of marriage!"

"Well, upon my word!" said Emma. "The young man will not lose anything for the want of asking."

"Then do you think I ought to refuse him?" said Harriet, looking down.

"Ought to refuse him! My dear Harriet, what do you mean? Are you in any doubt about that?"

"I didn't think that he loved me so very much," said Harriet; and then, after a pause, "but if you would just advise me . . . It will be safer to say 'No' perhaps. Do you think I had better say 'No'?"

"I cannot advise you, Harriet. You must be the best judge of what will make you happy. If you like Mr. Martin better than every other person, if you think him the most pleasant man you have ever been in company with, why should you delay? You blush, Harriet. Do you think of anyone else at this moment from whom you would rather receive an offer of marriage?"

Harriet did not answer, but after some minutes she said, "Miss Woodhouse, as you will not advise me I must do as well as I can by myself. I have now quite decided to refuse Mr. Martin. Do you think I am right?"

"Perfectly, perfectly right, my dearest Harriet; you are doing just as you ought, and I am indeed glad at this, for it would have grieved me to lose you as a friend. That must have happened if you had married Mr. Martin, for I could not have visited Mrs. Martin of Abbey-Mill Farm; but now I am sure of you for ever."

"You could not have visited me!" cried Harriet. "I never thought of that before! That would have been too dreadful! What an escape! Dear Miss Woodhouse, I would not give up the pleasure and honour of your friendship for anything in the world."

Eight

THE REPLY

Harriet had now to consider the reply she must make to Mr. Martin's letter. Emma advised her to write it at once: "You will need no help from me, Harriet." But when Harriet read Mr. Martin's letter again she said, "I did not know that he loved me so much." Emma thought that if the young man had come in at that moment, she would have agreed to marry him after all.

The letter was written—with more advice from Emma than she had intended to give; but she saw that Harriet would need her support in making a suitable reply. Emma's help was, in fact, given in every line of the letter.

When the letter was sent off, Harriet said, rather sadly, "I shall never be invited to Abbey-Mill again."

"I could never bear to part with you if you were," said Emma. "You are a great deal too necessary at Hartfield to be spared to Abbey-Mill."

A little later Harriet said, "Now he has got my letter; I wonder what they are all doing, and whether his sisters know. If he is unhappy, they will be unhappy too. I hope he will not mind it so very much."

"Let us think of those among our friends who are more

likely to be happy," said Emma. "Perhaps at this moment Mr. Elton is showing your picture to his mother and sisters."

"My picture! But by this time he has left it at the picture-framer's."

"I do not think so, Harriet. He will not go to the picture-framer until to-morrow morning. To-night he will treasure the picture. He will show it with delight to his family. They will ask many questions about you. They will wish to know your name. How interested and how happy they will all be!"

Harriet smiled. The thought of Mr. Elton occupied in this way was certainly cheering.

Nine

A SURPRISE FOR MR. KNIGHTLEY

Harriet slept at Hartfield that night. Next morning she went to Mrs. Goddard for an hour or two; but it was arranged that she should return to Hartfield for a visit of some days.

While she was gone Mr. George Knightley came. He and Emma talked together while Mr. Woodhouse took a short walk in the garden.

To Emma's surprise, Mr. Knightley began speaking about Harriet—and with more praise than he usually did.

"She is a pretty girl," he said, "and in good hands she will grow into a valuable woman."

"I am glad you think so; and I hope that she will have the help she needs."

"Come!" he said, "you wish to be praised, so I will tell you that you have improved her."

"Thank you. I should be sorry, indeed, if I did not think I had been of some use. And praise from *you* is very welcome. I do not often have it!"

"Are you expecting Miss Smith again this morning—"

"Yes, almost at once; she has been gone longer than she intended."

Mr. Knightley smiled. "I think I may perhaps know the reason for her delay," he said. "I have good reason to believe that your little friend may have found an important letter for her at Mrs. Goddard's."

"Indeed! What sort of letter?"

"I have reason to think," he replied, "that Harriet Smith has received an offer of marriage from an excellent man, Robert Martin. He is very much in love and he means to marry her."

"That is very kind of him," said Emma, "but is he sure that Harriet means to marry him?"

"Well, well, he has made her an offer—at least, I think he may have done so this morning. He came to ask my opinion, and I advised him to marry. I praised the fair lady too, and sent him away very happy. He probably went to Mrs. Goddard's this morning."

"Tell me, Mr. Knightley, how do you know that Mr. Martin did not make his offer yesterday?"

He looked surprised. "Certainly, it is possible."

"Come," said she, "I will tell you something in return for what you have told me. Mr. Martin did make his offer yesterday—and he was refused."

Mr. Knightley stood up looking very angry. "Then she is a greater fool than I thought," he said. "What does the silly girl mean?"

"Oh, of course," said Emma, "a man can never understand when a woman refuses an offer of marriage. A man always imagines that a woman will accept anyone who asks her."

"Nonsense! A man does not imagine any such thing. But what is the meaning of this? Harriet Smith refuse Robert Martin! Madness, if it is so; but I hope you are mistaken."

"I saw her answer; nothing could be clearer."

"You saw her answer! You wrote her answer too. Emma, *you* told her to refuse him."

"No; but if I did, I should not feel that I had done wrong. Mr. Martin is a very respectable young man, but I cannot admit that he is Harriet's equal."

"Not Harriet's equal!" cried Mr. Knightley loudly and

warmly. "No, he is not her equal, for he is as much above her in good sense as he is in rank of life. Emma, you are blinded by your love for that girl. Who is she? No one knows who her parents are. She has no respectable relations. She has been taught nothing useful. She is pretty and good-tempered, and that is all. When Robert Martin spoke to me about her I had some doubts, because I felt that the gain was all on her side; but I could not change the views of a man who was so much in love. I knew that everyone would think Harriet a very lucky girl. I felt sure that you would be glad. I remember saying to myself, 'Emma will be pleased at this, for she will see how fortunate it is for Harriet'."

"It is strange that you should know so little of Emma as to say any such thing. Harriet is my close friend. Could I wish her to marry a man whose family I cannot visit?"

Mr. Knightley did not answer her question. He said, "You have been no friend to Harriet, Emma. She was very happy with the Martins before she became your friend. She would have been very happy as Robert Martin's wife. I always thought that the friendship between yourself and Harriet was foolish, but I kept my thoughts to myself. I now see that it has been very unfortunate for Harriet."

"We think so differently on this point," said Emma, "that it is useless to talk about it any longer. We shall only be making each other more angry."

Mr. Knightley was certainly angry. "Good morning to you," he said, and quickly walked away.

Ten

MR. AND MRS. JOHN KNIGHTLEY

For some weeks after the events of the last chapter, Emma could not do much to help Mr. Elton in his courting of Harriet. Harriet's picture, excellently framed, was hung up in the sitting-room at Hartfield and was much admired by all who came to the house. But Emma and her father were thinking of the visitors they expected from London—"poor Isabella" with her husband, Mr. John Knightley, and their five children.

Mr. John Knightley was the brother of Mr. George Knightley, whom we have already met. His wife, Isabella, was Emma's elder sister.

Mrs. John Knightley was a pretty little woman with gentle, quiet manners. She was a good wife and mother, and could never see a fault in her husband or in any of her children. Mr. John Knightley was a successful lawyer and a good husband. He was a tall, gentlemanly man, but was sometimes impatient in his manners. As his wife worshipped him so much, it was not likely that he would be cured of this fault.

On the evening of their first day at Hartfield, Mr. Woodhouse naturally talked of "poor Miss Taylor." "It is a sad business," he said.

"Oh yes, sir," said Isabella. "How you must miss her! And dear Emma, too. I have been so grieved for you both. Do you see Mr. and Mrs. Weston fairly often?"

Mr. Woodhouse hesitated. "Not so often, my dear, as we should wish."

"Oh, father," said Emma, "we have only missed seeing them on one day since they were married. They are very kind in visiting us so often."

"That is just as it should be," said John Knightley. "I have always told you, my love," he said, turning to his wife, "that the change would not be felt so much as you feared."

"It is true," said Mr. Woodhouse, "that poor Mrs. Weston does come and see us fairly often. But then she always has to go away again."

"It would be very hard upon Mr. Weston if she did not," said Emma. "Mr. Weston is such an excellent man that he deserves to be cared for by a good wife."

"And where is the young man?" asked John Knightley. He was speaking of Mr. Weston's son by his first wife. This son did not live with his father. When his mother died, he went to live with her sister, a rich woman who lived in the North of England. He had been given his *aunt's* name and was now known as Frank Weston Churchill.

"He has not been here yet," said Emma. "We all hoped that he would come to his father's marriage, but he could not come because his aunt was ill."

"But you should tell them of the letter, my dear," said Mr. Woodhouse. "He wrote a letter to poor Mrs. Weston when she married Mr. Weston—a very kind letter. She showed it to me. I thought it a very good letter indeed. I cannot tell whether it was his own idea. He is young, and his aunt perhaps——"

"My dear father," said Emma, "he is twenty-three. You forget how time passes."

"Twenty-three! Is he, indeed. I should have not thought it. And he was only two years old when his poor mother died. I remember the letter very well. It was written from Weymouth and it began, 'My dear Madam'. I forget how it went on, but it was signed 'F. C. Weston Churchill'. I remember it perfectly."

"How very pleasant and proper of him," said Mrs. John Knightley. "I have no doubt that he is an excellent young man. But how sad it is that he does not live at home with his father. I could never understand how Mr. Weston could part with him."

"No doubt he thought it would be best for his son," said John Knightley. "The Churchills are rich, and Mr. Weston is a cheerful, good-tempered man. He would be contented not to see his son often if he could know that he would be well provided for."

At this moment Mr. George Knightley came in. Emma hoped that he and she might now be friends again.

When he took one of the children in his arms, Emma said, "What a comfort it is that we think alike about these children. We often differ in our opinions about men and women, but about the children we always agree."

"If you would think of men and women in the natural way in which you think of these children, we might always think alike," he replied.

"You always think that *I* am in the wrong," said Emma.

He smiled at her, and said, "Yes, and there is good reason. I was sixteen years old when you were born."

Eleven

MR. ELTON TRIES TO PLEASE

There could not be a happier woman in the world than Mrs. John Knightley during this short visit to Hartfield. Every morning she went with her five children to see her old friends in Highbury, and every evening she talked to her father and sister about all she had done. She could wish for nothing except that the days would not pass so quickly.

On the second day of the visit Mr. Weston came to Hartfield to ask his friends there to come and dine at his house, Randalls, on the next day. Mr. Woodhouse was frightened at first of going so far, and of coming back after dark. He wished Emma and Mr. and Mrs. John Knightley to go; yet he did not want to be separated from them, even for one evening. He agreed at last that the journey would not be too difficult. There were two carriages, his own and the one in which Mr. and Mrs. John Knightley had come from London. Mr. Woodhouse, with his daughter, Isabella, and Harriet, would go in the first carriage. Emma and John Knightley would follow in the second. Mr. Weston said that it would be a small party. The only other guests would be Mr. Elton and Mr. George Knightley.

On the day before this great event (for it was a great event for Mr. Woodhouse to dine out in December) Harriet came to Hartfield as usual; but she soon found that she had a bad cold. She got worse as the day went on, and, not wishing to give trouble at Hartfield, she went back to Mrs. Goddard's, to be nursed by her.

Emma went to see her on the next morning and found that Harriet's cold was worse. She was feverish, and she had a sore throat. She agreed, with many tears, that she could not possibly go to the party.

Emma sat with her as long as she could, and she tried to comfort Harriet by telling her how sad Mr. Elton would be when he found that she could not be at the party, and how much all the other guests would miss her.

As Emma left Mrs. Goddard's door, she met Mr. Elton coming towards it. He greeted her warmly and said, "I heard that Miss Smith was ill, and I came to enquire about her, so that I might bring the news to you at Hartfield."

"That was very kind," said Emma. "I am afraid that my poor friend is worse. She is feverish, and she has a sore throat."

"A sore throat!" he cried. "Not catching, I hope. Has the doctor seen her? Indeed, you should take care of yourself as well as of your friend. Let me advise you to run no risks."

Emma was not frightened for herself but she rather wished to increase Mr. Elton's fears for her friend; and she felt that as Harriet could not go to the party, he might perhaps be too unhappy to go himself.

"Mr. Elton," she said, "the weather is very cold, and you do not look well. Would it not be best for you to stay at home and take care of yourself to-night?"

Mr. Elton looked as if he did not know what to say. Fortunately for him, at this moment Mr. John Knightley came up. He, with his two eldest boys, had been visiting his brother at Donwell Abbey.

"I have been trying to persuade Mr. Elton," said Emma, "that, as the weather is so cold and he does not look well, he should not come to Randalls to-night. I think he should take care of himself."

"If the weather is the only difficulty," said Mr. John Knightley, "Mr. Elton is welcome to a seat in my carriage. We will call for him at his house."

To Emma's great surprise, Mr. Elton at once accepted this invitation. "Well," she said to herself, "this is most strange."

Soon afterwards Mr. Elton left them. Before going, he said to Emma, "Miss Woodhouse, I shall go to Mrs. Goddard's this afternoon for further news of your friend, and I hope that I shall bring good news when I have the happiness of seeing you this evening."

When he went away John Knightley said to Emma, "I never in my life met a man who took such trouble to please the ladies as Mr. Elton does. He is sensible enough with men, but with women he is quite silly."

"Mr Elton's manners are not perfect," said Emma, "but when a man tries so hard to please, one can forgive a great deal."

"Yes, Emma, and everyone must see that he certainly does his best to please *you*."

"Me!" said Emma with great surprise. "Are you thinking that Mr. Elton is in love with *me*? What an idea!"

"I confess that such an idea has come to me. I speak as a friend, Emma. I believe he may think that you like him. You had better think about it and decide what you mean to do."

"I thank you," said Emma, "but you are certainly quite mistaken. Mr. Elton and I are very good friends, and nothing more." She walked on, amusing herself with the thought of the silly mistakes which people who think they are wise often make in their judgment of others. John Knightley said no more.

Twelve

JOHN KNIGHTLEY IS BAD-TEMPERED

Mr. Woodhouse had so completely made up his mind to the visit that he set out quite happily in spite of the cold weather. He was too full of the wonder of his going to notice that it was cold, and too warmly clothed to feel it. It was, however, very cold, and before the second carriage started some snow was coming down and it seemed likely that more would follow.

When Emma entered the second carriage with John Knightley, she soon found that he was in a bad temper. He disliked leaving his children in order to spend the evening in another house, and he expected no pleasure from the visit.

"A man must have a very good opinion of himself," he said, "when he asks people to leave their own home on such a day as this in order to have the pleasure of coming to see him. I could not do such a thing; it is extremely silly. At this moment it is actually snowing, and we are going to spend five hours in another man's house with nothing to say or to hear that was not said and heard yesterday and may not be said and heard tomorrow. And we are going in bad weather, to return probably in worse."

Emma did not reply She could not agree to all he said—as his wife would have done. She could not, like Isabella, meet all his bad temper with a smile and with "Very true, my love." But she did not wish to quarrel with him; so she remained silent.

The carriage stopped at Mr. Elton's house. He entered it immediately and the party set out again for Randalls.

Mr. Elton was extremely cheerful. Emma thought that he must have received good news of Harriet, but when she asked him about her, his face lengthened at once, and in a low voice he said:

"I was on the point of telling you, Miss Woodhouse. I called at Mrs. Goddard's and I was grieved to find that Miss Smith is not better, but rather worse."

"How unfortunate this is," said Emma, "and it will be such a sad loss to our party to-day."

"Sad, indeed. She will be missed every moment."

This was said with a sigh, which Emma was glad to hear, but she thought that it should have lasted longer; and she was greatly surprised when, a moment later, Mr. Elton began to talk cheerfully of other things.

"Mr. and Mrs. Weston are charming people," he said; "they are so friendly and so kind. It will be a small party, but when small parties are of the right people, they are far better than large ones. You, perhaps, do not agree with this, Mr. Knightley, for you are used to the large parties of London."

"Sir," said John Knightley, "I know nothing of the large parties of London. I never dine with anybody."

"Indeed!" said Mr. Elton in a voice of wonder and pity, "I had no idea that the lawyers were such slaves to their work. Well, sir, the time must come when you will be paid for all this, when you will have little labour and much enjoyment."

"My first enjoyment," John Knightley replied, as the carriage passed through Mr. Weston's gate, "will be to find myself back at Hartfield again."

Thirteen

AT RANDALLS

When Emma and her two companions entered the sitting-room at Randalls, Mr. Woodhouse and Isabella had been there for some time. Harriet's cold was well talked over, and Emma hoped that she might be allowed to forget for a time both Harriet and the strange behaviour of Mr. Elton.

This did not happen, however, for Mr. Elton took a place beside her, and his behaviour was such that she could not help asking herself the question—"Can it be possible that John Knightley is right, and that this foolish man is beginning to love me instead of Harriet? How dreadful if it is so!"

Mr. Elton was so anxious that she should be perfectly warm; he talked with so much interest about her father; and he praised her pictures so warmly, but with so little knowledge, that Emma felt it difficult to preserve her good manners. She did so for Harriet's sake, still hoping that all would be well; but she found it difficult to go on talking to Mr. Elton because something was being said at the other end of the room which she badly wanted to hear. Mr. Weston was speaking about his son, Frank Weston Churchill. She heard the words "my son" and "Frank" repeated several times, and she thought that Mr. Weston must be saying that he expected a visit from his son. But before she could stop Mr. Elton, Mr. Weston began to talk of something else.

Emma was sorry, for although she often said to herself that she would never marry, there was something in the name of Mr. Frank Churchill which always interested her. Since his father had married Miss Taylor she had often thought that if she *were* to marry, he was the very person to suit her, in age and in other ways. The friendship between her family and the Westons seemed to make it suitable, and she felt certain that the idea had come to Mr. and Mrs. Weston. She had, therefore, a great curiosity to see Mr. Frank Churchill.

This being so, it was difficult for Emma even to pretend to listen to Mr. Elton. She could only hope that the subject of Frank Churchill's visit would be talked of again later in the evening. And in this she was not mistaken. Emma found herself sitting next to Mr. Weston at dinner, and quite soon he said to her:

"We want only two more to be just the right number. I should like to see your pretty little friend, Miss Smith, and my son. You perhaps heard me saying that we are expecting Frank. He hopes to be with us in two weeks."

Emma agreed with him that the presence of Miss Smith and Mr. Frank Churchill would make the party quite complete.

"How great a pleasure it will be to you and to dear Mrs. Weston to see your son."

"Yes, indeed," said Mr. Weston, "but Mrs. Weston will not allow herself to hope for Frank's coming, in case he should again be prevented. He has those to please who must be pleased, and who (between ourselves) can sometimes only be pleased at the cost of a good many sacrifices."

"I am sorry that there should be any doubt about the matter," said Emma, "but I am on your side, Mr. Weston. I think he will come."

Fourteen

SNOW

The evening passed pleasantly enough, but Mr. Woodhouse was soon ready for his coffee, and after drinking his coffee he was ready to go home. But John Knightley, who had been out to look at the weather, came back with the news that the ground was covered with snow and that it was still snowing.

Poor Mr. Woodhouse was much alarmed. He was silent with fear, but all the others had much to say. Some were surprised and some were not surprised. Some had a question to ask and some had comfort to offer.

Emma did her best to cheer her father and to prevent him from hearing what John Knightley was saying. But that was impossible. John Knightley went on in a loud voice:

"I very much admired your courage, sir, in coming out in such weather, for, of course, you saw that it was going to snow very soon. Everybody must have seen the snow coming on. I admired your spirit, and I hope we shall get home all right. We have two carriages, and if one of them is overturned in the snow, the other will be near at hand. No doubt we shall all be safe at Hartfield by midnight."

"You had better order the carriage at once, my love," said his wife. "No doubt we shall be able to get along if we set out at once. I am not at all afraid. If we do come to anything bad I could get out and walk. I can change my shoes, you know, the moment I get home; and that is not the sort of thing that gives me a cold."

"Indeed!" he replied. "That is the most extraordinary thing in the world. My dear Isabella, you know very well that usually everything gives you a cold. Walk home! It will be bad enough for the horses."

At this moment Mr. George Knightley entered the room. He had gone out immediately when he heard his brother's report, and he came back with good news.

"My dear sir," he said to Mr. Woodhouse, "there is no cause for alarm. I went out beyond the gate, and the snow is nowhere more than an inch deep. In some places it is hardly enough to whiten the ground; and it seems likely that it will soon be over. I have seen the drivers, and they are both agreed that there will be no difficulty in getting home."

Everyone was very glad; but nothing could satisfy Mr. Woodhouse that it would be safe to stay any longer.

Mr. George Knightley said to Emma, "Your father will not be happy till you start. Why do you not go?"

"I am ready, if the others are."

"Shall I ring the bell for the servant?"

"Yes, do."

So the bell was rung and the carriage ordered. Emma hoped that in a few minutes one of the two companions with whom she, was to travel back would be set down at his own house, and that the other would recover his temper when this troublesome visit was over.

Fifteen

EMMA AND MR. ELTON

When the first carriage came to the door, Isabella stepped in after her father. John Knightley forgot that he was to go in the other carriage; he stepped in, very naturally, after his wife. The carriage drove off, and as the second carriage came to the door Emma found, to her surprise, that she and Mr. Elton were to travel in it alone.

It was a difficult moment. If it had been yesterday, Emma would have been glad of the chance of talking to Mr. Elton about Harriet; but now she would rather that this had not happened. She believed that he had been drinking too much of Mr. Weston's good wine, and she felt sure that he would want to be talking nonsense.

She began, however, to speak of Harriet, and said how **sad** it was that poor Harriet could not come to the pleasant **party** they had just left.

Mr. Elton cut her short. To her great surprise he seized her hand and began making love to her.

"Dearest Miss Woodhouse," he said, "you must know of the feeling I have long had for you, and you will not blame me for taking this wonderful chance of telling you how much I love you."

It was really so! Mr. Elton, the lover of Harriet, was pretending to be in love with her, and actually asking her to marry him.

Emma was very angry, but she felt that much of this was due to the wine which Mr. Elton had drunk. In an hour from now he would be ashamed of himself. She therefore controlled her anger and spoke to him as gently as she could:

"I am very much surprised, Mr. Elton. You forget yourself—you mistake me for my friend. I shall be happy to deliver any message you may send to Miss Smith; but no more of this to *me*, please."

"Miss Smith!" cried Mr. Elton. "Message to Miss Smith! What can you possibly mean?"

"Mr. Elton," said Emma, "your behaviour is most extraordinary. I can only explain it in one way. You are not yourself, or you would not speak to me in this manner."

Mr. Elton had only drunk enough wine to raise his spirits and to give him courage—not enough to confuse his mind. He was perfectly clear as to what he wanted to say.

"Miss Smith!" he repeated. "I never thought of Miss Smith in that way in the whole course of my life, and I never cared for her but as your friend. If she has fancied otherwise, her wishes have misled her, and I am very sorry. But Miss Smith, indeed! Who can think of Miss Smith when Miss Woodhouse is near?"

Emma could mistake his meaning no longer.

"Mr. Elton," she said, "I am sorry that you have been giving way to any such feelings about me. Nothing could be

MR. ELTON LEAVES THE CARRIAGE WITHOUT SAYING GOODNIGHT

more opposite to my wishes. I have no thought of marriage at present. I was glad to see you so often at Hartfield because I thought that you were interested in my friend Harriet. Your pursuit of her (as I thought) gave me great pleasure, and I wished you success. Am I now to suppose that you never thought seriously of her?"

"Never, madam; never, I assure you. *I* think seriously of Miss Smith! Miss Smith is a very good sort of girl, and I wish her well. No doubt there are some who might not object to—. Everybody has their place. But as for myself, I need not, I think, so much despair of marriage with an equal as to think of marrying Miss Smith. No, madam, my visits to Hartfield were for yourself only, and the encouragement I received——"

"Encouragement!" cried Emma. "I gave you no encouragement. I have seen you only as the admirer of my friend."

They were now both very angry, and it was fortunate that at this moment the carriage stopped at Mr. Elton's door.

He stepped out without saying good-night. The carriage started again.

"Poor Harriet," thought Emma; "poor Harriet." She was very unhappy when she arrived at Hartfield.

Sixteen

EMMA LEARNS HER LESSON

Emma was welcomed with great pleasure by her father, who was anxious for her safety in the last part of her drive. When she arrived everyone seemed happy. John Knightley, ashamed of his bad temper, was now pleasant and kind. The day was ending in peace and comfort to all their little party except herself.

With great difficulty Emma tried to seem cheerful until the usual hour of going to bed. When she reached her own room she sat down to think and to be sad.

"It is a dreadful business," she said to herself. "It is the end of everything I wished for, and the beginning of all that I do not want. Such a blow for Harriet—that is the worst of all. I should not be so much ashamed of the mistakes I have made if Harriet did not have to suffer for them. If I had not led Harriet into liking Mr. Elton, I should not have been much troubled by Mr. Elton's foolish admiration of me."

Emma did not believe that Mr. Elton was really in love with her. "He wants to marry well," she thought, "and, knowing that I am rich, he pretended to be in love. He gave me plenty of fine words and sighs; but they did not sound like real love. He wants a rich wife, and since he cannot have me he will soon try someone else."

And then Emma thought again of Harriet. "I have talked poor Harriet into being in love with this man! She might never have thought of him but for me. How much I wish **that** I had been satisfied with urging her not to accept **Robert** Martin. I was quite right in that, but I ought not to have attempted more."

Before Emma went to sleep she had quite decided that it was foolish and wrong to try to bring any two people together. "I have learned my lesson." she thought, "and I shall never try to do anything of the kind again."

Seventeen

HARRIET'S TEARS

In the morning, fortunately for Emma, the ground was white with snow; and for some days she could not go out into the village. When the snow melted Mr. and Mrs. Knightley, with their five children, returned to London. On the same day a letter came to Mr. Woodhouse from Mr. Elton. "My dear Sir," he wrote, "I am leaving Highbury to-morrow morning for Bath, and I shall be spending several weeks there with friends. I am very sorry that, owing to the bad weather, I cannot come to see you before I go. I write, therefore, to say goodbye, and to send you my warm thanks for the pleasure which I have so often had from my visits to you."

Emma's name was not mentioned. Mr. Elton's anger with her could not have been more plainly shown. Emma was afraid that her father would notice it; but he was so surprised at Mr. Elton's sudden journey, and so much afraid that he would never come safely to the end of it, that he could think of nothing else.

Emma was very glad to know that Mr. Elton would be away from Highbury for a time. It was better for Harriet that she would have no chance of meeting him at present. Emma heard that Harriet's cold was better, and she thought that the time had now come when she must destroy all Harriet's hopes of marrying Mr. Elton. It was difficult enough to do this, but still more difficult to tell Harriet the real reason for Mr. Elton's frequent visits to Hartfield.

When Emma went to Mrs. Goddard's, she found that Harriet was better in health, but still very sorry at not going to Mr. and Mrs. Weston's party. Emma then told Harriet the sad story of what happened in the carriage when she was returning from the party with Mr. Elton.

Harriet cried a great deal. It was plain that she was deeply in love with Mr. Elton, but, in spite of this, she bore the news very well.

"Dear Miss Woodhouse," she said, "nobody is to blame. I always thought that I could not deserve the love of such a man as Mr. Elton. It was only your love for me that led you to think that it was possible."

Emma kissed her friend sadly, but gratefully, and came away.

Eighteen

MRS. AND MISS BATES

Emma now felt that she must see Harriet as often as possible, and that she must do all that she could to help Harriet to forget Mr. Elton. It was good for them both that Mr. Elton was still at Bath, so that they could not meet him in the streets of Highbury. When the weather improved, Emma and Harriet often went walks together, and sometimes they went to see friends in the village. One morning they visited Mrs. and Miss Bates.

Mrs. Bates was a very old lady who lived with her daughter in poor lodgings over a shop in the village street. They had very little money, but they were very happy. Everybody in the village loved Miss Bates, for she loved everybody, and was interested in everything. She thought herself a most fortunate creature, with an excellent mother and so many good neighbours and friends. She talked a great deal about little things, and Emma was of the opinion that she often talked too much. But Emma hoped that the company of someone who was always so cheerful would help to drive the thought of Mr. Elton from Harriet's head.

As they came near to Mrs. Bates's door Emma said, "Let us hope that we shall escape hearing her read out a letter from Jane Fairfax."

Jane Fairfax was a granddaughter of Mrs. Bates. Her mother—Mrs. Bates's youngest daughter—married Captain Fairfax, who was killed in saving the life of another officer, Colonel Campbell. Jane's mother soon died, and Colonel and Mrs. Campbell offered to bring up Jane with their own daughter until she was old enough to earn her living as a governess. Mrs. and Miss Bates gladly accepted this offer. They were sorry that Jane could not live with them, but Jane wrote long letters to her grandmother and her aunt, and Miss Bates often read the letters to friends who visited them.

When Emma and Harriet entered, they were warmly welcomed by the two ladies. Mrs. Bates, a very old lady, sat with her needlework in the warmest corner of the room. Her daughter almost overcame them with kindness—with thanks for their visit, care for their shoes, questions about Mr. Woodhouse, and offers of coffee and cake.

The name of Jane Fairfax was soon mentioned and Emma felt that she could not help asking, "Have you heard from Miss Fairfax lately?"

"Indeed we have," said Miss Bates. "We had a letter this morning."

"I hope she is well."

"Thank you; you are so kind. She is not as well as we could wish. But you shall hear the letter. It cannot be far off. Oh! here it is, just where I put it, under my work-basket. I knew it could not be far off, for I have been reading it again to my mother. A letter from Jane is such a pleasure to her that she can never hear it too often. And this letter contains such good news. Jane hopes to be here quite soon."

"Indeed, that must be a very great pleasure."

"Thank you. You are very kind. It is a pleasure indeed. Everybody is so surprised; but, as this letter tells us, the Campbells are going to Ireland on a visit to their daughter, who has just married Mr. Dixon—a very charming young man. Jane was asked to go with them, but she has not been well, and her kind friends, the Campbells, thought that it would be best for her to come home to the place where she was born. She was with the Campbells at Weymouth, but even the sea air did not do her much good."

"I think that her coming to you is an excellent arrangement," said Emma.

"Yes, indeed," said Miss Bates, "for nobody can nurse her as we can do. She is coming on Friday or Saturday. It is so sudden. You may guess, dear Miss Woodhouse, how excited I am. Well, now; you must hear the letter."

"I am afraid we must be running away," said Emma, looking at Harriet. "My father will be expecting us. When we came I had no intention of staying more than five minutes. I came in only because I could not pass your door without seeing Mrs. Bates. I have been so pleasantly delayed, but now we must wish you and Mrs. Bates good morning."

And not all that Miss Bates said could persuade Emma to stay longer. She reached the street, happy in this, that although she had heard all the news contained in Jane Fairfax's letter, she had been able to escape the letter itself.

Nineteen

AN EXCITING PIECE OF NEWS

Jane Fairfax arrived, and Miss Bates soon brought her to visit Mr. Woodhouse and Emma at Hartfield. On the morning of the visit, Emma and her father were talking about Jane.

"She is a very pretty and well-behaved young lady," said Mr. Woodhouse. "I shall be glad to see her again."

"Yes," said Emma, "she is very clever and beautiful. She has been well educated, and she has lived as an equal in Colonel Campbell's family; but soon she will have to earn her living. She will have to teach young children in some rich person's family. I do feel sorry for her!"

Mr. George Knightley, who had just come in, was pleased when he heard Emma speaking so kindly about Jane Fairfax.

"Yes," he said, "it is sad, indeed, that she must look forward to such a hard and uninteresting life; but Colonel Campbell cannot provide for her. He must think of his own daughter; and Mrs. and Miss Bates are very poor."

"Yes," said Mr. Woodhouse, "I am very sorry for them; and I have often wished to help—but one must always be so careful not to hurt their feelings. One can only send them sometimes a small present from the garden or the farm which may help them."

Mr. Knightley then said to Emma, "I have a piece of news for you. You like news, and I heard some on my way here which I think will interest you."

"News! Oh, yes, I always like news. What is it?—Why do you smile so?—Where did you hear it?—at Randalls?"

He had only time to say, "No, not at Randalls; I have not been near Randalls," when the door was opened and Miss Bates and Miss Fairfax walked into the room. Mr. Knightley saw at once that he had lost his chance.

Miss Bates began at once, "Oh, my dear sir, how are you this morning? You see I have brought our dear Jane to see you. Have you heard the news? Mr. Elton is going to be married."

Emma, who was shaking hands with Miss Fairfax, was so completely surprised that she could not help blushing.

"This is my news," said Mr. Knightley, looking at Emma with a smile. "I thought it would interest you."

"But where did *you* hear it?" cried Miss Bates. "Where could you possibly hear it, Mr. Knightley? For it is not five minutes since I heard it from Mrs. Cole—no, it cannot be more than five—or at least ten—for I was just ready to come out. And just at that moment Mrs. Cole came in and told us the news. A Miss Hawkins—that's all I know—a Miss Hawkins of Bath. But, Mr. Knightley, how could you possibly have heard it?"

"I went to see Mr. Cole on business an hour ago," said Mr. Knightley, "and he had just received Mr. Elton's letter."

"Well," said Miss Bates, "I suppose there was never a more interesting piece of news. Well, my dear Jane, we must be running away. It looks as if it might rain, and grandmama will be anxious. You must not be out in a shower. We think the air of Highbury has made her look better already. We do, indeed. Good morning to you, my dear sir, and to you, dear Miss Woodhouse. This has been a most interesting piece of news indeed."

At last Miss Bates and Miss Fairfax went away. Mr. Knightley went with them, and Emma was alone with her father.

Twenty

HARRIET MEETS OLD FRIENDS

"What a pity it is," said Mr. Woodhouse, when the visitors had gone, "that young people are in such a hurry to marry, and that they so often marry people whom they don't really know. Mr. Elton is a very young man. He only went away a few weeks ago, and what can he know of Miss Hawkins?"

Emma just managed to say, "Perhaps he knew her before, father;" but she was too busy with her own thoughts to pay much attention to what Mr. Woodhouse was saying.

"Mr. Elton to be married!" she thought. "In one way this is an amusing and a very welcome piece of news. His 'love'

HARRIET SEES THE MARTINS IN FORD'S SHOP

for me cannot have made him suffer very long. But poor Harriet! She will feel it. I hope that she will not hear the news suddenly on her way here. Perhaps she will meet Miss Bates; but she may have taken shelter from the rain."

The shower was heavy, but short. Soon after it was over Harriet came in. She looked unhappy, as if she had already heard the news.

"Oh! Miss Woodhouse," she said, "what do you think has happened?"

Emma felt that, as the blow had fallen, she could not show Harriet greater kindness than by listening. Harriet told her story very rapidly: "I started from Mrs. Goddard's half an hour ago. I was afraid that it might rain, but I thought that I could get to Hartfield first, and I walked as fast as I could, but just as I was passing Ford's shop, it began to rain very heavily, so I ran into the shop to take shelter. Mrs. Ford was very kind. She gave me a chair; and while I sat there, who do you think came in?"

Emma saw that Harriet's story was going to be different from the one she expected. Without waiting for a reply, Harriet ran on—

"Elizabeth Martin and her brother! I thought I should have fainted. I did not know what to do. I was sitting near the door, and Elizabeth saw me at once, but *he* did not; he was busy with his umbrella. I am sure that she saw me, but she looked away and took no notice. And they both went to the farther end of the shop, and I kept on sitting near the door. Oh dear, I was so unhappy. I could not go away, you know, because of the rain; but I wished to be anywhere in the world but there. Well, at last he looked round and saw me, and they began whispering to one another. I am sure they were talking about me. I could not help thinking that he was asking her to speak to me. Do you think he was, Miss Woodhouse?"

Before Emma could reply, Harriet went on, "She came and asked me how I was, and she seemed ready to shake hands, if I would. She did not do it as she used to do; I could see that she was changed, but she seemed to *try* to be friendly, and we shook hands, and stood talking for some time. But I don't know what I said. I remember she said, 'I am sorry we never meet now,' which I thought was almost too kind. Dear Miss Woodhouse, I was so unhappy. It had almost stopped raining and I wanted to get away—and then—only think!—I saw him coming towards me—slowly, you know, as if he did not quite know what to do. And so he came and spoke—very kindly—and I answered; but I have no idea of what I said; but at last I saw that the rain had stopped and I told him that I must go. Oh, Miss Woodhouse, I would rather have done anything than let this happen; and yet, you know, one could not help feeling glad when he behaved so kindly and pleasantly. And Elizabeth, too. Oh, Miss Woodhouse, do talk to me and make me comfortable again."

Emma wished that she could do so, but it was not easy, for she was not very comfortable herself.

"It was certainly an unfortunate experience," she said; "but the young man and his sister seem to have behaved well. Such a thing may never happen again, and therefore you need not think any more about it."

Harriet said, "Very true," but she still talked of it, and would talk of nothing else. Emma then told Harriet the news about Mr. Elton, hoping that it would help to drive the Martins out of her head.

At first Harriet did not seem to be very interested. The news did not pain her as it would have done yesterday. But soon her interest in Mr. Elton returned, and she began to talk about this fortunate Miss Hawkins who would soon be Mrs. Elton. Emma began to feel that perhaps Harriet's meeting with the Martins was a good thing. It would help her to get over the idea of Mr. Elton's marriage.

Twenty-one

THE HAPPINESS OF MR. ELTON

When Mr. Elton returned to Highbury he was a very happy man. He was angry and unhappy when he went away. He had failed in his attempt to get Miss Woodhouse as his wife, and he was insulted by her hopes that he would marry Miss Smith. He came back pleased with himself and with the world. He now cared nothing for Miss Woodhouse, and less than nothing for Miss Smith.

Emma soon found that Harriet was still in love with Mr. Elton. "I talked her into love," she thought sadly, "but I cannot so easily talk her out of it. Harriet is one of those girls who, when they once begin, will always be in love. Nothing will cure her of her love for Mr. Elton but another——" But here Emma stopped suddenly. She remembered the night on which she said to herself, 'I have learned my lesson. I shall never attempt anything of the kind again.' "But something must be done," she thought. "Harriet is very unhappy, and when Mr. Elton comes back to Highbury she cannot help seeing him every day. People are always talking about him and his coming marriage. They speak of the beautiful Miss Hawkins, and of how very much Mr. Elton is in love."

One day when Harriet came to Hartfield, she told Emma that Elizabeth Martin had come to Mrs. Goddard's and left a letter for her.

"It was not the sort of letter I used to receive from her," said Harriet, "but it was a kind letter in a way, and she said she hoped that we might sometimes see one another again."

This seemed to make Harriet more cheerful; but on the next day she was so unlucky as to see Mr. Elton at the very moment when he was setting out for Bath to be married, and this brought all her unhappiness back again.

Emma decided that it would perhaps be good for Harriet to return Elizabeth's visit by going for a very short time to Abbey-Mill Farm.

"Harriet must not run any risk of becoming friends with the Martins again," she thought. "That is quite impossible—and Harriet would not wish it. The best plan will be for me to take her in the carriage and leave her at Abbey-Mill Farm for a short time while I drive on a little further. Then I will come for her again—of course without going in. This will show the Martins that they must not expect to see much of Harriet now that she is my friend."

Emma was not quite satisfied with this arrangement. "It is perhaps not very kind to the Martins," she thought, "but I must do the best I can for Harriet, and a visit to Abbey-Mill Farm will help her to forget Mr. Elton for a time."

Twenty-two

A VISIT TO ABBEY-MILL FARM

When the day came for the visit, Harriet was not at all eager to go. During the drive she spoke several times about Mr. Elton. "In four days from now he will be married," she said. "How happy he and Miss Hawkins must be!"

When they came to the farm, and Harriet was put down at the end of the long path which led to the front door, Emma saw her looking round, as if old memories were coming back. Emma decided that the visit must certainly not last longer than a quarter of an hour. She went on and paid a short visit to an old servant who was married, and now lived in Donwell village. She was back again exactly at the appointed time.

When Harriet came down the path towards the carriage, Emma was glad to see that she was alone. No alarming young man was with her. Miss Martin was standing at the front door of the farm, but she did not wait to see the carriage drive away.

Harriet was too much troubled by the visit to be able to give a clear account of it.

"Oh! Miss Woodhouse," she said, "it was so strange to be back again. It seemed that none of us knew quite what to do. I only saw Mrs. Martin and the two girls. At first we were all dreadfully stiff and unfriendly. We talked almost all the time just as if we had never been happy together; but at last Mrs. Martin said that she thought that I had grown taller, and she spoke of an evening last summer when Mr. Martin measured me and his sisters, and made pencil-marks on the wall to show how tall we were. The marks were still there, and I was just going to stand against the wall so that we might see whether Mrs. Martin was right, when the servant came to tell us that you were back again. I am sure they felt how short my visit was, and they remembered that last summer I was with them for six weeks. They did not seem happy when I came away, and I was not happy myself. Oh! Miss Woodhouse, how difficult everything is!"

Emma was very much inclined to agree with Harriet. She was quite tired of both Mr. Elton and the Martins. She decided to go home by way of Randalls, and to visit Mr. and Mrs. Weston. The sight of those two happy people would do them both good.

When the carriage drove up to the door of Randalls the servant who came out said, "Mr. and Mrs. Weston are not at home. They have been out some time. I think they have gone to Hartfield."

"This is too bad!" said Emma, as they turned away. "And now we shall just miss them. I do not know when I have been so sorry." She sat back in the carriage, looking very unhappy.

But soon the carriage stopped. She looked up and saw that it was stopped by Mr. and Mrs. Weston, who were standing to speak to her.

"Good news!" cried Mr. Weston. "We have just been telling it to your father. Frank comes to-morrow."

There was no resisting such news. There seemed to be no doubt that it was true. Mrs. Weston's happy face showed that she now felt sure that Frank would come.

"He is at Oxford today," said Mr. Weston, "and tomorrow he will be here. I shall bring him up to Hartfield very soon."

"My father and I will be very pleased to see him," said Emma.

"You must not expect such a *very* fine young man," said Mr. Weston. "You have only had *my* account, you know—and I am his father. Perhaps he is really nothing extraordinary." But Mr. Weston's smile showed what he really thought about Frank. Emma felt also that he and Mrs. Weston had some secret hopes about herself and Frank which they tried to hide—though not very successfully.

The carriage drove on, and Emma was now in good spirits. The sadness which she felt after Harriet's visit to the Martins passed away. Even Harriet seemed a little happier, and she did not once mention either the Martins or Mr. Elton before Emma left her at Mrs. Goddard's door.

Twenty-three

FRANK CHURCHILL

Frank Weston Churchill arrived a day earlier than he was expected. On the morning after Emma heard that he was coming, she entered the sitting-room and saw two gentlemen sitting with her father—Mr. Weston and his son. They had been there only a few minutes. Mr. Weston was still explaining why Frank arrived a day before his time, and Mr. Woodhouse was still in the middle of his very kind welcome. The visitors rose when Emma entered, and Frank was presented to her.

Emma did not think that too much had been said in his praise. She said to herself, "He is certainly a *very* good-looking young man. I think that I shall like him, and he seems already to like me."

Mr. Weston said, "It did not surprise me that he came yesterday instead of today. One cannot go slowly upon a journey. When I was a young man I was just the same. It is always a pleasure to come to one's friends earlier than they expect us."

"Yes, sir," said Frank; "there are some houses in which one could not do this, because it might cause trouble; but in coming *home* I felt I might do anything."

Emma saw how pleased Mr. Weston was when Frank spoke of Randalls as "home." "The young man knows how to make himself pleasant," she thought.

Later, when their two fathers were talking together, Frank spoke to her about Mrs. Weston. Emma was glad of this, for she wanted to know what he thought of her friend.

"I knew," he said, "that she was a well-educated woman, and I expected that she would have pleasant manners. But, considering everything, I expected only a fairly good-looking woman, no longer young. It was a great surprise to me, therefore, to see such a pretty young woman."

Emma laughed. "You cannot praise Mrs. Weston too highly

to *me*," she said, "but do not let her know that you have spoken of her as a pretty young woman."

Mr. Weston began to move. "I must go," he said. "I have business at the Crown Inn, and many things to buy at Ford's for Mrs. Weston. But do not let me hurry you, Frank. You need not come with me." But Frank was too well-mannered to stay longer. He immediately rose and said,

"As you are going further on business, sir, I will take the chance of paying a visit which I must pay some time or other." Then, turning to Emma, he continued, "I happened to meet at Weymouth a lady who is, I think, a near neighbour of yours—a Miss Fairfax; though Fairfax is not, I believe, the right name. I should have said Barnes or Bates. Do you know any family of that name?"

"Indeed we do," said Mr. Weston. "Mrs. Bates—we passed her house—I saw Miss Bates at the window. I remember now that you said you had met Miss Fairfax at Weymouth."

Frank seemed to hesitate. "It is not really necessary that I should go today," he said. "I could go another day, but——"

"Oh, go today, go today," said his father. "What is right to be done cannot be done too soon. And I must tell you, Frank, that *here* you should be careful to show every proper attention to Miss Fairfax. You saw her with the Campbells. They are rich people and she lived with them as an equal. But here she is with a poor old grandmother who has hardly enough money to live on. If you do not visit them early they will feel hurt."

Frank seemed to agree with his father and they went away together.

"He has grown to be a very fine young man," said Mr. Woodhouse.

"Yes, father," said Emma, "and it was very pleasant to hear him speak so kindly of dear Mrs. Weston. We can now think of them all as being very happy together at Randalls, at any hour of the day."

Twenty-four

A MORNING WALK

Next morning Frank and Mrs. Weston came together to Hartfield. Emma was pleased to see that they were already becoming friends. They came to ask Emma to join them in a walk round the village, which she was very glad to do.

Frank asked to be shown a house in which his father and his grandfather lived for many years. Mrs. Weston then remembered that an old woman who was Frank's nurse when he was a baby was still alive, and Frank immediately wished to pay her a friendly visit. Emma thought that these things showed his character in a pleasant light.

They then came to the Crown Inn. The house was very old, but Frank noticed that one large room was almost new. He asked about this, and was told that the room was built some years ago for dancing.

"At that time," said Mrs. Weston, "there was much dancing in Highbury and a large room was wanted for it, but the custom seems to have passed. The room is now only used as a club for the gentlemen—and half-gentlemen—of Highbury."

Frank was immediately interested. He looked at the room through a window, which was open.

"Miss Woodhouse," he said, "I am sure that you can do anything in Highbury. Why do you not start the dances again? In the winter they should be held at least once a month."

Emma did not consider this very seriously, but it was some time before he was willing to move on.

When they passed the house in which Mrs. and Miss Bates lived, Emma said to Frank, "Did you visit them here yesterday?"

"Oh, yes," he replied. "I was just going to tell you. A very successful visit. I saw all the three ladies. But you should have warned me about the talking aunt! She made me stay much longer than I intended. I told my father that I would

FRANK LOOKS AT THE ROOM AT THE CROWN INN

be at home before him, but it was impossible to get away; and when at last he came to look for me I was surprised to find that I had been sitting with them for nearly an hour."

"And how did you think Miss Fairfax was looking?"

"I cannot say that she was looking well—not so well as when we used occasionally to meet at Weymouth."

"You knew the Campbells at Weymouth?"

"Yes, I knew them well. Colonel Campbell is a very charming man, and Mrs. Campbell is a friendly, warm-hearted woman."

"You know what they have done for Miss Fairfax, and that soon she will have to do something for herself? She is to be a governess."

"You get on to tender subjects, Emma," said Mrs. Weston, smiling. "Please remember that I am here, and that I have been a governess. I will move a little further off."

"I certainly do not forget to think of *her*," Emma said to

Frank, "but I always think of her as my friend—my dearest friend."

When they were all together again Frank said, "My father tells me that you love music. Did you ever hear Miss Fairfax play?"

"Ever hear her!" said Emma, "you forget how much she belongs to Highbury. I have heard her every year since we both began to learn. She plays beautifully; but, of course, she and Miss Campbell always had very good teachers. Colonel Campbell has done a great deal for Miss Fairfax. You

know, I expect, that her father saved his life, and in doing so lost his own?"

"Yes, I heard the story at Weymouth," he said. "I always thought that Miss Fairfax played well. It was a pleasure to hear her. What a pity it is that her grandmother has no piano."

"Yes," said Emma, "but when she is in Highbury, people who have a piano are always very pleased if she will come and play."

They were now passing Mr. Elton's house. It was not a large house—not as large as Randalls, and much smaller than Hartfield.

"You have heard us speak of Mr. Elton," said Mrs. Weston. "He has gone to Bath to be married, and he will soon return with a rich wife. She may perhaps think that the house is rather small."

"It is surely quite large enough," said Frank. "If two people love one another they do not want a large house."

Mrs. Weston laughed. "You do not know what you are talking about," she said. "You are used to your uncle's large house at Enscombe, and you do not know how difficult it is to live comfortably in a small one." He laughed in reply, and said that he could live very happily in Mr. Elton's house.

Emma thought, "When his uncle and aunt die he will be the owner of Enscombe, and he will be very rich. But they may live a long time, and he seems to think that if he falls in love he will wish to marry early, and he will not mind living in a small house."

Twenty-five

FRANK HAS HIS HAIR CUT

On the next morning Mr. and Mrs. Weston called at Hartfield, and Emma could not help feeling sorry when she found that Frank was not with them.

"You will be surprised to hear the reason," said Mrs. Weston—rather sadly, Emma thought. "He has gone to London to get his hair cut. He said at breakfast that he must go, and he sent at once to the Crown for a carriage."

Emma shared in her friend's sadness. After the good opinion of Frank which she formed yesterday, it was sad to find that he could act so foolishly and hastily. "How can he be so silly," she thought, "as to drive sixteen miles to London, and back again, only to have his hair cut? It is not kind to Mrs. Weston," and, after a moment, she allowed herself to add, "it is not kind to me."

But Mr. Weston excused his son. "He is on a holiday," he said, "away from his aunt, who is very strict with him; he enjoys his freedom, and he must be allowed to do as he likes."

Except for the unpleasant news which they brought concerning Frank, Emma was very glad to see Mr. and Mrs. Weston, for she wished to have their advice on an important matter. On that morning she and her father had received an invitation to an evening party at the Coles. Of course Mr.

Woodhouse could not go; but the question whether Emma should go was very difficult.

The Coles had lived for some years in Highbury. They were a very good sort of people, simple and friendly. Emma felt that Mr. Cole was not a gentleman like her father, or the two Mr. Knightleys, or even like Mr. Elton. She knew that Mr. Elton sometimes dined with the Coles, but she always thought worse of him for doing so.

The Coles were becoming richer, for their business in London was doing well. They now lived in a larger house, and they were giving larger parties. Emma did not expect that they would be so brave as to invite her and her father; but they had now done so. She badly wanted the advice of Mr. and Mrs. Weston on the question as to whether she should go.

"My dear Emma," said Mrs. Weston, "of course you must go. We are all going. Frank is so much looking forward to it. He says it is probable that there will be dancing. The Coles have a room in their new house which is quite large enough. And there will certainly be music. You and Jane Fairfax will have to play. The Coles have a beautiful piano."

"My dear," said Mr. Woodhouse, "I think you had better go. I, of course, cannot go. You must explain that I do not go out in the evening, but please thank Mr. and Mrs. Cole for so kindly inviting me. Perhaps one of our kind friends will come and keep me company on that evening. Ah! Miss Taylor, if you had not married you would have stayed at home with me."

"Well, sir," said Mr. Weston, "as I took Miss Taylor away, I must find someone to take her place. If you wish, I will go at once to Mrs. Goddard, and ask if she is able to come and keep you company on the night of the party."

"That will be very kind of you," said Mr. Woodhouse; "but please tell Mrs. Goddard that I shall not trouble her to stay longer than she wishes. Emma, my dear, you will not, I am sure, be staying late."

"But, father, you do not wish me to come away before I am tired?"

"Oh, no, my dear; but you will soon be tired. There will be a great many people talking at once. You will not like the noise."

"But, my dear sir," cried Mr. Weston, "if Emma comes away early it will be breaking up the party."

"And no great harm if it does," said Mr. Woodhouse. "The sooner every party breaks up the better."

"But you do not consider what the Coles will think if Emma leaves their party early. Others will follow her and it will quite spoil the party. I am sure, sir, that you do not wish Emma to disappoint the Coles—good, friendly people who have been your neighbours for ten years."

"No, indeed, I do not. I should be very sorry to give them any pain; and I am grateful to you for warning me, Mr. Weston. I know what worthy people they are. My dear Emma, we must consider this. I am sure that, if your coming away early will cause pain to Mr. and Mrs. Cole, you will not mind staying a little longer. You will be perfectly safe, you know, among your friends."

"Oh, yes, father. I have no fear for myself. I am only thinking of you. But I am sure that you will be comfortable with Mrs. Goddard. And you must promise me that, when she goes home, you will not sit up for me."

Mr. Woodhouse promised, and Emma accepted the invitation, with more pleasure than she would have thought possible a month ago.

Twenty-six

THE MYSTERY OF THE PIANO

When, on the day of the party, Emma's carriage drove up to the Cole's front door, it was followed by another, and Emma was pleased to find that this second carriage was Mr. George Knightley's. Mr. Knightley did not often use his carriage—he preferred walking. He kept no carriage-horses at Donwell Abbey, and when he needed them he hired them from the Crown Inn. He now helped Emma down from her carriage. As he did so Emma said, "I am glad to see that you have come to the party like a gentleman—in your carriage. I always know when you have walked to a party, and I am always ashamed of you; but now I am happy to go into the party with you."

"Foolish girl!" he replied, but not at all in anger.

Emma had as much reason to be satisfied with the rest of the party as with Mr. Knightley. The Coles received her with a great deal of kindness and respect. When the Westons arrived, they at once came to her with the kindest looks of admiration and love. Frank followed eagerly, in a way which showed pleasure at meeting her again. She found that he was sitting next to her at dinner, and she felt sure that he had done something to make this happen.

The party was rather large. It included a few neighbours whom Emma knew slightly, and Mr. Cox, the lawyer, with his wife. Other members of the Cox family, with Miss Bates, Jane Fairfax and Harriet Smith were to come later in the evening.

Already, at dinner, the party was too large for general talk, and while others were talking about politics or about Mr. Elton—and wondering what Mrs. Elton would be like—Emma could give all her attention to Frank. Soon, however, she heard something being said at the other end of the table which interested her, and she tried to listen to it.

Mrs. Cole was speaking: she said, "Have you heard of the wonderful present which Miss Fairfax has received? I visited Mrs. Bates this morning, and when I entered her room the first thing I saw was a beautiful piano. It arrived from London yesterday, quite as a surprise, for neither Miss Fairfax nor her aunt or grandmother knew anything about it. They think that it must be a present from Colonel Campbell, who is now in Ireland."

All who heard this news rejoiced at it, and Mrs. Cole went on: "I do not know when I have heard anything which has given me more pleasure. It always has quite hurt me that Jane Fairfax, who plays so beautifully, has no piano, especially when we know so many houses where there is a fine piano which is quite wasted. For example, there is our own piano, a very good one. I cannot play it, and our little girls are only beginning to learn." Here Mrs. Cole looked down the table to where Emma and Frank were sitting, and said, "We are hoping that Miss Woodhouse will give us the pleasure of hearing her play this evening."

Emma bowed, and made a suitable reply. She then turned to Frank Churchill and said, "You told me, I think, that you often heard Miss Fairfax play at Weymouth?"

"Yes, indeed; she gave great pleasure to all the members of our party. I remember that Mr. Dixon, who has now married Miss Campbell, seemed to prefer the playing of Miss Fairfax even to that of the young lady he was going to marry. Sometimes I thought that Miss Campbell did not quite like it."

"But Miss Fairfax and Miss Campbell were great friends. They were brought up together."

"Yes," said Frank, "they were—and no doubt still are— great friends."

Emma's imagination was beginning to be active. A strong suspicion entered her mind.

"Is it possible," she said, "that the piano is the gift of Mrs. Dixon—or, indeed, of Mr. and Mrs. Dixon; for you say that Mr. Dixon was a great admirer of Miss Fairfax's playing?"

"Yes," he said, "I do think that it is possible. And there is a further reason for Mr. Dixon's interest in his wife's friend— and for her interest in him. He saved her life. We were all out in a boat. In a sudden wind, Miss Fairfax was almost blown into the sea; but Mr. Dixon caught her. It was the work of a moment."

All Emma's suspicions were made stronger. She looked very thoughtful for a time, and then she said, "I am sure that the piano is the gift of Mr. and Mrs. Dixon—perhaps only of Mr. Dixon."

"You may be right," he said, with a smile; "I think you see more deeply into such matters than I do. Yes, it may be so. The piano may well be—an offering of love."

Twenty-seven

MRS. WESTON TAKES TO MATCH-MAKING

When dinner was over, the ladies went to the sitting-room leaving the gentlemen to their wine. It was not long before the other ladies arrived. Harriet came in, nicely dressed, and looking very pretty. Emma was glad to see that she looked happy. Harriet clearly meant to enjoy the party and to forget, for a time, the pain of disappointed love.

Then Miss Bates and Miss Fairfax came in. Emma looked at Jane, and she thought, "Jane is much more beautiful than Harriet, and she has far better manners. It is clear that she has lived all her life with well-educated and well-mannered people, which Harriet has only done since I brought her to Hartfield. But Harriet is the more fortunate of the two. It is surely better for Harriet to love even Mr. Elton in vain, than for Jane Fairfax to have the dangerous pleasure of knowing that she is loved by the husband of her friend."

In so large a party it was not necessary for Emma to speak to Jane Fairfax. She did not wish to speak of the piano—she felt that she was too much in the secret of it to be able to show curiosity or interest. But she saw that others were telling Jane how pleased they were to hear that she now had a piano, and she saw the blush (was it a blush of shame?) with which Jane spoke of "my excellent friend, Colonel Campbell".

When the gentlemen came to the sitting-room, Frank Churchill soon came to sit by Emma.

"I have made a dreadful discovery," he said. "I have been here a week to-morrow—half my time. I never knew the days fly so fast. A week to-morrow! And I have only just begun to enjoy myself."

"Perhaps you may now begin to be sorry that you spent one whole day in getting your hair cut."

"No," he said, smiling, "I am not at all sorry about that. I have no pleasure in seeing my friends unless I am fit to be seen."

Soon afterwards Emma noticed that he was looking very keenly at Jane Fairfax, who was at the other end of the room. At last he said, "Miss Woodhouse, perhaps you will kindly excuse me for a few minutes. I feel that I shall seem ill-mannered if I do not speak to Miss Fairfax, after I met her at Weymouth."

He went immediately; and Emma soon saw him standing in front of Miss Fairfax and talking to her. Before he could return to his chair, it was taken by Mrs. Weston.

"My dear Emma," said Mrs. Weston, "I have been wishing to talk to you. I have been making discoveries and forming plans, just like yourself, and I must tell you about them at once. Do you know how Miss Bates and her *niece* came here?"

"How!—Surely they were invited, as we were."

"Oh yes, they were invited, but how did they get here?"

"They walked, I expect. How else could they come?"

"Very true; I thought so myself. But when I saw Jane Fairfax here I thought she looked ill, and I could not bear the idea of her walking home again. So, as soon as Mr. Weston came into the room, and I could get at him, I asked him to offer to drive Miss Bates and her niece home. He, of course, agreed at once; but when I went to tell Miss Bates, she replied —of course with very many thanks—that our kindness was unnecessary, for Mr. Knightley's carriage brought them to the party and will take them home again. And I suspect, Emma, that it was for this reason that he hired a pair of horses. For, as you know, he usually walks."

"Very likely," said Emma; "nothing more likely. Mr. Knightley is exactly the man to do such a thing. I know he had horses to-day, for we arrived together; and I laughed at him about it, but he said nothing to explain why he did not walk."

"Well, Emma," said Mrs. Weston, smiling, "I have thought of an explanation. The more I think of it, the more probable it appears. In short, I have made a match between Mr. George Knightley and Jane Fairfax. See the result of keeping you company! What do you say to it?'

"George Knightley and Jane Fairfax!" Emma exclaimed. "Dear Mrs. Weston, how could you think of such a thing? George Knightley must not marry. When he dies—which we all hope will be many, many years hence—Donwell Abbey must go to John Knightley's and dear Isabella's son, little Henry. I cannot allow George Knightley to marry anyone; and I am sure it is not at all likely. And Jane Fairfax! How could you think of such a thing?"

"Well, she has always been a favourite with him, as you know very well."

"Only in the way of friendship," said Emma, "and because he is sorry for her. And, as you know, he has a great respect for Mrs. and Miss Bates; he is glad to show them any kindness, quite apart from Jane Fairfax. My dear Mrs. Weston, please do not take to match-making. You do it very badly. Jane Fairfax married to the owner of Donwell Abbey! What a dreadful idea! No, no, no; for his own sake I would not have him do such a thing."

"Well, Emma," said Mrs. Weston, "I have not yet given up my idea—and I have another reason for it, which I have not yet mentioned. *Somebody* has sent Jane a piano. We have all thought of it as a present from Colonel Campbell, although Jane admits that there was no mention of it in his last letter to her. I cannot help suspecting that it was Mr. Knightley who sent it."

"I think it most unlikely," said Emma. "Even if he loved her he would not make a secret of such a gift. It is a most unlikely thing for him to do, for he never does anything mysteriously."

"Well, I have often heard him say how sad it is that Jane has no piano."

"Mrs. Weston," said Emma, "you take up an idea and run away with it, as you have often blamed me for doing. I see not the slightest reason to suppose that Mr. Knightley is in love with Jane Fairfax, and I do not for one moment think that he gave her the piano."

Twenty-eight

MUSIC AND DANCING

The talk between Emma and Mrs. Weston was now stopped, for coffee was brought in. When it was over, the piano was opened and Mrs. Cole came to ask Emma to play. Frank Churchill, who had found a chair next to Miss Fairfax, came with Mrs. Cole and eagerly supported her.

Emma agreed at once, for she knew that she could neither play nor sing as well as Jane Fairfax, and she thought that this would be less noticed if she played first and Jane followed. She chose a simple song, which she knew that she could sing well—a song which people always liked. She sang another song, written for two voices, with Frank Churchill. He sang softly and correctly. At the end he said, "I am afraid I am no great singer," but it was clear that he had given pleasure.

"Your voice," Emma said, "is delightful; it must certainly have been well trained."

Emma now took a chair at some distance from the piano. Frank remained with Jane Fairfax and he played the piano for her songs. Soon Mr. Knightley, who was standing near the piano, looked back at Emma, and he then came and sat down by her. They talked first of Jane's singing, and Mr. Knightley's praise was certainly warm. Emma thought that she would not have noticed it before her talk with Mrs. Weston, but in order to test Mrs. Weston's suspicion, she said, "Jane is very fortunate to have received this gift of a piano from Colonel Campbell."

"Yes," he replied, "but surprises are foolish things, and it is often troublesome to receive presents in this way. I should have expected Colonel Campbell to have more sense."

From the way in which he spoke, Emma felt quite certain that was not Mr. Knightley who gave the piano to Jane Fairfax.

When Jane had sung several songs, Mr. Knightley began to show some anxiety about her. She looked tired, but Mrs. Cole

was asking her to sing again—"just once more." Frank
Churchill said, "I think you could sing this song for two voices
without tiring yourself too much. Your part of it is easy. Most
of the work falls upon the other singer. Let us sing it
together."

Mr. Knightley grew angry. "That fellow," he said, "thinks
of nothing but of showing off his own voice." He went up to
Miss Bates and said, "Miss Bates, are you mad to let Miss
Fairfax tire herself in this way? They have no mercy on her.
Please go and put a stop to it." Miss Bates did so at once. In
her real anxiety for Jane, she could hardly stay to say how grateful she was to Mr. Knightley, but stepped forward at once and
put an end to all further singing.

A few minutes later, dancing was mentioned and the idea
was warmly taken up by all the young people. The room was
cleared to make space, and Mrs. Weston, who played country
dances very well, sat down at the piano. Frank Churchill
came forward with great eagerness to ask Emma to dance with
him. She bowed, and he at once led her into the dance.

Emma looked round, when she could do so, to see if Mr.
Knightley was dancing. Usually he did not dance, and Emma
thought that, if he now asked Jane Fairfax to dance with him,
it might mean something. But no; he was talking to Mrs. Cole,
and Jane was dancing with somebody else.

Two dances were all that could be allowed. The time was
getting late and Miss Bates was anxious to get home because
of her mother. After some attempts, therefore, to be allowed
to begin again, the young people could only look sorrowful,
and thank Mrs. Weston for the pleasure she had already given
them.

Frank Churchill went with Emma to her carriage.

"Perhaps it is just as well," he said to her, "that there was
not more dancing. I must have asked Miss Fairfax to dance
and her dancing would not have pleased me after yours."

Twenty-nine

HARRIET GOES SHOPPING

Emma was not sorry that she went to the Coles' party. She had many happy memories of it on the next day. But perfect happiness, even in memory, is not quite common, and there were two subjects on which she was not quite happy. She felt that she had been wrong in allowing Frank Churchill to know of her suspicions about Jane Fairfax. . This was perhaps failing in the duty which one woman owes to another. Her other cause for regret also concerned Jane Fairfax. Emma was very sorry that she had not made better use of her music lessons and that she had not spent more time in practising; for she knew that it was for this reason that she could neither play nor sing as well as Jane Fairfax. She felt this so strongly that she sat down at once and practised for two hours.

She was at last stopped by the arrival of Harriet, and if Harriet's praise could have satisfied her she might soon have been comforted.

"Oh, if I could only play as well as you and Miss Fairfax!" said Harriet.

"Do not class us together, Harriet. My playing is no more like hers than a lamp is like sunlight."

"Well, I shall always think that you play as well as she does, or if there is any difference nobody would find it out. Besides, if Miss Fairfax does play so very well, you know, it is what she must do because she will have to teach. The Coxes were wondering last night whether she would get into any great family. How did you think the Coxes looked?"

"Just as they always do—rather ill-mannered."

"They told me something," said Harriet, rather hesitatingly.

Emma felt that she must ask what this 'something' was, although she was afraid that it might refer to Mr. Elton.

"They told me that Mr. Martin dined with them last Saturday."

"Oh!"

"He came to see their father on some business, and Mr. Cox asked him to stay to dinner."

"Oh!"

"They talked a great deal about him, especially Anne Cox. I do not know what she meant, but she asked me, 'Do you think that you will go and stay with the Martins again next summer'?"

"She showed bad-mannered curiosity, just as one would expect Anne Cox to do."

"She said that he was very pleasant the day he dined there. He sat by her at dinner. Miss Nash—one of the teachers at Mrs. Goddard's—says that she thinks either of the Coxes would be very glad to marry him."

"Very likely; I think they are, without exception, the most foolish and ill-mannered girls in Highbury."

Harriet did not answer; but she said that she must go, for she had business at Ford's. Emma thought it best to go with her. Another accidental meeting with the Martins was possible, and in Harriet's present state it might be dangerous.

When they entered Mrs. Ford's shop, Harriet was a long time in making up her mind what to buy. Emma grew tired of waiting, and she went to the door of the shop to watch what was happening in the village street. Nothing very exciting happened, even in the busiest part of Highbury. Dr. Perry walked hastily by. Across the road Mr. Cox was letting himself in at his office door. Then there was an old man with a donkey, a woman going home from shopping with a full basket, two dogs fighting over a bone, and some children looking eagerly at some cakes in a shop window.

Then Emma looked down the road, towards Randalls. Two persons appeared—Mrs. Weston and Frank Churchill. Emma felt that, after the party last night, this was a very pleasant meeting, and it was clear that Frank Churchill felt this also.

"We were walking to Hartfield," said Mrs. Weston, "but Frank tells me that last night I promised Miss Bates that I would visit her this morning in order to see the new piano. I have quite forgotten that I did, but Frank seems so sure of it that I think I had better go. I am going now."

Frank turned to Emma and said, "While Mrs. Weston is paying her visit I hope I may be allowed to walk to Hartfield with you—and to wait for Mrs. Weston there?"

Mrs. Weston looked disappointed. "But Frank," she said, "I thought you were coming with me. I am sure that they will be very pleased to see you—and you have not yet seen the piano."

"I did not intend to go to-day," he said. "The room is very small. And I think I would be a nuisance. But perhaps I would be a nuisance here: Miss Woodhouse looks as if she did not want me!"

Emma laughed. "I am here with Miss Smith," she said. "She takes a long time over her shopping, and I must wait for her. You had better go with Mrs. Weston and hear the piano."

"Well, if you advise it."

"Do come with me," said Mrs. Weston. "We need not stay long, and we can go to Hartfield afterwards. I really wish you to come with me, and I quite thought that you meant to do so."

He could say no more; and with the hope of Hartfield to reward him, he crossed the road with Mrs. Weston and knocked at Mrs. Bates's door.

Thirty

FRANK MAKES HIMSELF USEFUL

Harriet took a long time to decide upon the articles she wished to buy; and when she had made up her mind, there was the further question as to where the packets were to be sent —to Hartfield or to Mrs. Goddard's.

"Shall I send it to Mrs. Goddard's, Miss?" asked Mrs. Ford.

"Yes, please," said Harriet. "But, no; perhaps it had better go to Hartfield; but Mrs. Goddard will be anxious to see what I have brought. But I want *this* at once, at Hartfield. Perhaps you could send this to Hartfield and the other things to Mrs. Goddard's."

"It is not right to give Mrs. Ford the trouble of sending two parcels," said Emma.

"No trouble in the world, Madam," said Mrs. Ford.

"Miss Woodhouse, what would you advise?" Harriet asked.

"I advise that you do not give another moment's thought to the subject," said Emma. "To Hartfield, please, Mrs. Ford."

At this moment voices approached the shop. Mrs. Weston and Miss Bates met them at the door.

"My dear Miss Woodhouse," said Miss Bates, "I have just come to ask you and Miss Smith to come and sit down with us for a few minutes and see the piano."

Emma accepted this invitation for herself and her friend.

They now crossed the road, Miss Bates leading the way and still talking. She opened the front door of the house, and as the visitors walked upstairs she said, "Pray take care, Mrs. Weston, there is a step at the corner. Pray take care, Miss Woodhouse, our stairs are rather dark and narrow, I fear. Pray take care, Miss Smith."

They came to the top of the stairs without accident, and entered the little sitting-room.

A peaceful scene was before them. Frank sat at the table with the old lady's spectacles in his hands. He seemed to be trying to mend them. The old lady herself, being unable to

A PEACEFUL SCENE

work without them, was asleep in her chair near the fire; and Jane Fairfax was seated at the piano.

Although he was still busy with the spectacles, Frank greeted Emma eagerly, and he seemed very happy to meet her again. "You find me trying to be useful," he said. "Tell me if you think I shall succeed."

"What!" said Mrs. Weston, "have you not finished yet? You would not earn a living at this kind of work."

"I have not been working all the time you were away, for I have been helping Miss Fairfax to make the piano stand firm. The floor is not level, and, as you see, we have put paper under one of the legs."

Jane Fairfax was asked to play, and there was warm praise both for her and for the piano.

"Whoever Colonel Campbell employed to choose the piano," said Frank, "he certainly chose a good one."

Jane was still seated at the piano. She did not look round, and Frank smiled at Emma. He went on, "Colonel Campbell has excellent taste. No doubt he either gave his friend very careful directions, or he wrote to the piano-makers himself. Do you not think so, Miss Fairfax?"

Jane still did not look round, but it was possible that she did not hear, for Mrs. Weston was talking to her.

Emma whispered to Frank, "*Please* do not say any more. It will give her pain—and it is not fair. And please remember, mine was only a guess."

He shook his head with a smile, and looked as if he had very little doubt that her guess was right.

Soon afterwards Miss Bates, in passing near the window, saw Mr. Knightley on horseback not far off.

"There's Mr. Knightley," she said. "I must speak to him if possible, just to thank him. I will not open the window here; it will give you all colds. I will go to my mother's room. When he knows who is here, I expect he will come in."

She caught Mr. Knightley's attention, and all that they said to one another was easily heard by the visitors in the next room.

"Good morning. How do you do?" "Very well, thank you." "So many thanks for the carriage last night. Do come in. You will find some friends here."

"How is your niece, Miss Bates? How is Miss Fairfax? I hope she did not catch a cold last night."

Mrs. Weston smiled at Emma, but Emma shook her head and smiled back.

Miss Bates was again saying, "So many thanks for the carriage last night," but Mr. Knightley cut her short and said, "I am going to Kingston. Can I do anything for you?"

"Oh dear!—Kingston;·are you? Mrs. Cole was saying the other day that she wanted something from Kingston."

"Mrs. Cole has servants to send. Can I do anything for *you*?"

"No, thank you. But do come in. Who do you think is here? Miss Woodhouse and Miss Smith. They were so kind as to come in and hear the piano. Do put up your horse at the Crown and come in."

"Well," he said, "Perhaps, for five minutes."

"Mrs. Weston and Mr. Frank Churchill are here too. Quite delightful; so many friends."

The tone of Mr. Knightley's voice changed at once.

"Your room is full enough," he said, "and I am in rather a hurry. I will call another day and hear the piano."

"Well, I am so sorry! Oh, Mr. Knightley, what a delightful party last night! Did you ever see such dancing? Miss Woodhouse and Mr. Frank Churchill; I never saw anything like it."

"Oh, very delightful, indeed," said Mr. Knightley. "I can say nothing less, for your visitors must be hearing everything I say." Then, raising his voice, he went on, "I do not see why Miss Fairfax should not be mentioned too. I think she dances very well, and I think that Mrs. Weston plays country dances better than anyone in England. Now, if your friends are kind, they will say something nice about you and me in return. But I cannot stop to hear it." He said good-bye and went off.

Emma now said that she and Harriet must go. The visit had lasted longer than any of them intended. Mrs. Weston and Frank also rose to go. They walked with Emma and Harriet as far as the Hartfield gates, and then set off for Randalls.

Thirty-one

AN EVENING AT RANDALLS

It may be possible to do without dancing entirely. Young people sometimes do not dance for many months together without seeming very much the worse. But when once a beginning is made, it is only very quiet young people who do not wish to go on.

Frank Churchill was far from being quiet. Having danced once at Highbury, he was eager to dance again; and he had not much difficulty in getting Emma to agree with him. Emma was quite willing that people in Highbury should see again how delightfully Miss Woodhouse and Mr. Frank Churchill could dance together. She knew that this was something in which she need not blush to measure herself beside Jane Fairfax.

The matter was talked over during the last half-hour of an evening which, rather to his own surprise, Mr. Woodhouse spent with his daughter at Randalls.

Frank said, "Let us have the same party here that we had at the Coles, the same people and"—bowing to Mrs. Weston—"the same excellent musician."

"But will there be room here for ten dancers?" said Mrs. Weston. "I really do not think there will."

"The doors of the two rooms are just opposite each other," said Frank. "Could we not use both rooms and dance across the passage? Then perhaps we could ask more people."

Mrs. Weston did not agree with Frank. "Where could we have supper?" she asked. And Mr. Woodhouse disagreed with it very strongly on the ground of health.

"You would all catch terrible colds," he said. "I could not bear it for Emma. Emma is not strong. She would catch a dreadful cold. So would poor little Harriet. So would you all."

It was clear that this idea must be given up. But Frank soon had another idea. "Why not hold our dance at the Crown," he said. "There is a large room there—you will remember, Miss Woodhouse, that I had the pleasure of looking at it in your company."

Mr. Woodhouse was still more alarmed at the thought of holding the dance at an inn. "An inn is always damp and dangerous," he said. "It would be far better to hold the dance at Randalls."

"But, sir," said Frank, "there is so much more room at the Crown that it would not be necessary to open any windows during the whole evening. And, as you know, sir, it is the dreadful habit of opening windows and of letting in the cold air upon heated bodies, which gives people colds. We should be so much less likely to catch colds at the Crown that the only person who would have reason to be sorry at our going there would be Dr. Perry."

"Sir," said Mr. Woodhouse warmly, "if you think that Dr. Perry is glad when people catch colds you are very much mistaken. Dr. Perry is very grieved when any of us are ill. And as to opening windows, sir, it is always wrong to do it. I do not think that you should decide about this dance in a hurry. There is plenty of time."

"But unfortunately," said Frank, "my own time is getting very short." He looked at Emma as though he needed her help.

"Come, father," she said, "we must talk about it when we get home. The Crown, you know, would be good for one thing. It would be so easy for the horses."

"Yes, my dear, that is true. Well, we will talk about it again."

Mr. Woodhouse always felt that if he could delay an event, there was a fair chance that it would never happen.

The carriage was ordered. He and Emma said good-night and set out for Hartfield.

Thirty-two

FRANK IS CALLED HOME

Frank Churchill got his way, and arrangements were made to hold the dance at the Crown. Emma found that she was looking forward to it with great pleasure. But there was one fear which troubled her—the fear that Frank Churchill would have to return to Enscombe before the date fixed for the dance. Mr. and Mrs. Weston found that there was so much to be done that they could not possibly fix a date before the end of the second week of Frank's holiday. Mr. Weston—always the more hopeful of the two—was quite sure that Mrs. Churchill would allow Frank to stay for the dance, although it would take place two days after the day on which he was expected home. Mrs. Weston was not quite so hopeful. She felt that a risk was being taken, and Emma quite agreed with her.

It was a necessary risk, for the arrangements could not be completed earlier. A letter was sent to Enscombe, asking that Frank might be allowed to remain for the dance.

The reply came, and although it was plain that Mrs. Churchill and her husband were not pleased with Frank, the permission was granted. All was now safe and hopeful. Emma could once more look forward with great pleasure to the dance.

One morning, when Mr. George Knightley came to Hartfield, Emma was sorry to find that he refused to be interested in the dance.

"If the Westons think it worth while to take all this trouble for a few hours of noisy pleasure," he said, "I have nothing to say against it, but they shall not choose my pleasures for me."

"But you will go to the dance?" said Emma.

"Oh, yes! I must be there, and I will keep as much awake as I can; but I would far rather be at home looking over William Larkin's weekly account."

"But have you no pleasure in seeing the dancing, Mr. Knightley, even if you do not dance yourself?"

"Pleasure in seeing the dancing!" he cried. "Not I. I never look at it. I do not know who does."

Emma thought that this was not very respectful either to her or to Jane Fairfax. "It is quite plain," she said to herself, "that in his feelings about the dance Mr. Knightley is not in any way agreeing with Jane Fairfax."

Emma had good reason for thinking this; for, a few days before, when she met Jane in the village street, Jane said, "Oh! Miss Woodhouse, I hope nothing will happen to prevent the dance. I do look forward to it, I confess, with very great pleasure."

"It is clear," Emma now thought, "that Mr. Knightley's lack of interest in the dance is a further sign that Mrs. Weston is wrong in thinking that he is in love with Jane. No doubt he has a great deal of friendship and sympathy for Jane—but no love."

There was soon no time for quarrelling with Mr. Knightley, and no further need to do so. A letter came from Mr. Churchill asking Frank to return immediately. "Your aunt is ill," Mr. Churchill wrote; "far too ill to do without you. She was not well when she wrote to you a few days ago; but she did not say so because, as you know, she never thinks of herself, and she did not wish to interfere with your pleasure. But now she is worse, and we both think it important that you should come home at once."

Mrs. Weston sent a note to Hartfield, telling Emma the sad news. "There is no doubt that Frank must go to-day," she wrote, "although he well knows the nature of his aunt's illnesses. They never happen but for her own comfort. After breakfast Frank will go into Highbury to say good-bye to the few friends he has there, and you may expect him at Hartfield quite soon."

This note put an end to Emma's breakfast. When once she had read it she could only sigh and complain. The loss of the party—the loss of the young man—and all that the young man might be feeling. It was too dreadful!—such a delightful evening as it would have been! Everybody so happy and she and Frank the happiest! "The only comfort I can have," she thought, "and it is a very small one—is that I said it would be so."

The feelings of Mr. Woodhouse were quite different. He thought mostly of Mrs. Churchill's illness. He wanted to know what it was, how she was treated, and what medicine she took.

"As for the dance, my dear Emma, I am of course very sorry that you will all lose so much pleasure, but there can be no doubt that you will be much safer at home."

Thirty-three

ALMOST A LOVE SCENE

Emma was ready for her visitor some time before he arrived; but it was plain from his sorrowful look that the fact that he was late was not due to any lack of eagerness to see her. His sorrow at leaving Highbury—and leaving *her*—seemed almost more than he could bear. He sat down, lost in thought, for a few minutes.

When he spoke, it was only to say, "Miss Woodhouse, of all unhappy things, saying 'Good-bye' is the worst."

"But you will come again," said Emma. "This is not your last visit to Highbury."

"Ah!" he said, shaking his head. "It is all so uncertain. If my uncle and aunt go to London early in the year, as they used sometimes to do, it would be much easier for me to come; but last year they did not go, and I am afraid the custom is gone for ever."

"Our poor dance must be given up."

"Ah! That dance!—Why did we wait for anything? Why not seize the pleasure at once? You told us it would be so. Oh! Miss Woodhouse, why are you always right?"

"Indeed, I am very sorry to be right now. I would much rather have been wrong."

"If I can come again, we are still to have our dance. My father and Mrs. Weston both say so; and please remember, Miss Woodhouse, that you and I are to have the first two dances together."

"I shall not forget it," said Emma.

"I have had such a lovely holiday," he continued. "Every day more precious and more delightful than the one before—every day making me less fit to bear any other place. Happy are those who can remain in Highbury."

"Since you are so fond of Highbury now," said Emma, "I will be so bold as to ask—why were you so long in coming? Do you find us better than you expected? I am sure you do; for I do not think that you expected much from us. If you had suspected Highbury of being as good a place as you have found it, you would have come long ago."

He laughed—rather uncomfortably, Emma thought—and he said that he did not agree with her; but Emma felt quite sure that she was right.

"And you must really be off this morning?"

"Yes; my father will join me here. We shall walk back together, and I must be off immediately. I am afraid that he will be here any moment."

"Not five minutes to spare, even for your friends Miss Fairfax and Miss Bates—not to mention the old lady? They will be sorry, indeed, not to see you."

"Oh, but I *have* been there. I was passing the door, and I thought I had better go in for a few minutes. Miss Bates was out, and I felt that I must wait until she came in. She is a woman at whom it is easy to laugh, but for whom one always has a great respect. I should have been sorry to leave Highbury without seeing her. But I came on here as soon as I could."

He hesitated, got up, and walked to the window. Emma felt that something important was coming—something which she was not sure that she wished to hear. She hardly knew what to say; but at last, forcing herself to speak, and speaking

D

as calmly as possible, she said, "You were quite right; I am
glad that you went to see them before coming here."

He looked at her, as if trying to read her thoughts. What
Emma thought was, "He is more in love with me than I
supposed."

At last he said, "Miss Woodhouse, you can hardly, I think,
be entirely without suspicion——" But at that moment the

ALMOST A LOVE SCENE

door opened and Mr. Weston came in, followed immediately
by Mr. Woodhouse.

The two young people controlled themselves and spoke as
naturally as they could. Their fathers noticed nothing, and
Mr. Weston soon said, "Now, Frank, it is time to go."

Frank rose to say good-bye. "I shall hear about you all,"
he said. "It is something that I can be sure of that. Mrs.
Weston has promised to write to me, and she will tell me
everything. In her letters I shall be at dear Highbury again."

A friendly shake of the hand, and a very warm "Good-bye" brought his speech to an end, and the door was soon shut on Frank Churchill.

How short the notice had been; and how short their meeting! "Only this morning," Emma thought, "we were all looking forward to the party. And now——!"

Thirty-four

EMMA IS NOT SURE THAT SHE IS IN LOVE

Emma soon found that there had been a very sad change in her life. She and Frank had been meeting one another almost every day since he arrived. His being at Randalls had added very greatly to the interest of her life. Every morning there was the hope of seeing him, and the growing belief that he was especially interested in her. He was full of life, and his manners were delightful. To complete every other recommendation, he had *almost* told her that he loved her.

"The question is," she said to herself, "am I—although I am determined never to marry, and never to leave my father —am I, just a little, in love with Frank Churchill?"

"I think that I must be," she went on. "This feeling that I am not interested in anything, that there is nothing in particular that I want to do, that everything is uninteresting about the house—surely all this shows that I am in love. It would be very strange if I were not—for a few weeks at least. Well, evil to some is always good to others. Many will be sorry that Frank has gone, and that the dance cannot be held. But Mr. Knightley will be very glad. He will now be able to spend the whole evening with William Larkin checking the accounts of his farm."

Mr. Knightley showed no unusual happiness. "I cannot say that I am sorry on my own account," he said, "but you,

Emma, who have so few chances of dancing, are really out of luck. I am very sorry for you."

Emma was quite sorry for herself. In a few days she began to have little doubt that she was in love. The only question was, how much? At first she thought that it was a good deal; but, in a week or two, only a little. She had great pleasure in hearing Frank Churchill talked of; and, for his sake, greater pleasure than ever in seeing Mr. and Mrs. Weston. She was very often thinking about him, and when Mrs. Weston received a letter, it gave Emma great pleasure to know how Frank was, whether his aunt's health was improving, and whether it was likely that Frank would be able to come to Highbury again soon.

"If he does," said Emma to herself, "I think I begin to see what will happen. We shall have some very pleasant times together. We shall have our dance at the Crown. He will show that he is very much in love with me, but when he tells me so, I shall refuse him." When she reached this point Emma decided that she could not be very much in love.

In a letter which Mrs. Weston received from Frank soon after he went away, he wrote, "When I left Highbury so suddenly, I had not a moment to spare for Miss Woodhouse's beautiful little friend." Emma had no doubt that this was all for herself. Harriet was remembered as being *her* friend. Frank asked Emma to make his excuses to Harriet and to give her a friendly message. Emma did this with pleasure, and she noted the pleasure with which Harriet received the message.

An idea began to enter Emma's head. It grew quickly as she decided that, after all, she was perhaps not very much in love with Frank. Frank was interested in Harriet. Emma knew that he was very much struck with the loveliness of Harriet's face and the charm of her simple manners.

"Is it altogether impossible," she thought, "that when I refuse Frank's offer of marriage, he may turn to my beautiful little friend?"

"I must not think too much about it," she said to herself.

"I know the danger of doing so. But more unlikely things have happened; and when Frank and I have ceased to care for one another as we do now, his love for Harriet would be a bond of friendship between him and me—a friendship of the kind to which I can already look forward with pleasure."

Emma was glad to have some comfort in store for Harriet, for Mr. Elton would soon return to Highbury bringing his bride with him.

Thirty-five

A MARRIAGE VISIT

Mrs. Elton was first seen in Church; but it is not easy, in such a place, to come to a satisfactory idea as to whether a young woman is very pretty indeed, or only rather pretty, or not pretty at all. The ladies of Highbury decided that, until they had visited Mrs. Elton in her new home, they could not form their opinions about her.

Emma knew that her own visit to Mrs. Elton would be very difficult—a great trial. She said to herself, "It will be best to go soon, and get it over; and in the end it will probably be best for Harriet if I take her with me. Now that Mr. Elton is back again she will see him almost every day. For three weeks she has had several reasons for not thinking so much about him—the coming of Frank Churchill, the party at the Coles, and the plans for the dance. But now she is unhappy again. She needs all the help that I can give her."

One day, when Harriet was talking a great deal about "Mr. Elton and his bride," Emma said, "You know, Harriet, when you talk in this way you make me feel very much ashamed of myself. You could not give me a greater proof of the mistake I fell into. It was all my doing, I know. I have not forgotten it. I deceived myself; and I deceived you. This will be a painful thought to me for ever."

Harriet could only murmur a few words in reply.

Emma continued, "It is for your own good—not for mine— that I ask you to try to think less about Mr. Elton, and to think more of your duty, your self-respect and your peace of

EMMA AND HARRIET VISIT MR. AND MRS. ELTON

mind. These are the thoughts which I have been pressing upon you. They are very important, and I am sorry that you cannot feel them enough to act upon them. It is less important that I myself should be saved from pain. But perhaps, Harriet, you will sometimes remember what would be kind to me."

This had more effect upon Harriet than anything else that Emma said.

"Oh! Miss Woodhouse," she replied, "you have been the best friend I have ever had. Nobody is equal to you. I care for nobody as I do for you. Oh! how ungrateful I have been!"

Emma now felt that she could safely ask Harriet to go with her to pay their marriage visit to Mrs. Elton.

The visit was, of course, short; and there were so many reasons for discomfort that Emma wished that it could have been even shorter. Harriet behaved very well, but she was rather white and silent. Emma would not allow herself to form an opinion of Mrs. Elton until she had seen her more often. Mrs. Elton was richly dressed, though perhaps not in the best taste. Emma felt that she did not really like her. She thought that as a bride, and also as a newcomer to the village, Mrs. Elton talked with too much freedom and boldness.

As for Mr. Elton, Emma said to herself, "His position is very difficult; he is in the same room with the woman he has married, the woman he wanted to marry, and the woman he was expected to marry. Perhaps he is making the best of it."

When they left the house, Harriet said, "Well, Miss Woodhouse, what do you think of her? Is she not charming?"

There was a little hesitation in Emma's answer. Oh! yes—very—a very pleasant young woman."

"I think her beautiful—quite beautiful."

"Very well dressed, indeed."

"I am not at all surprised," said Harriet, rather sadly, "that he fell in love with her."

"Oh! No. There is no reason for surprise. She is rich, and she came in his way."

"I expect," said Harriet, "that she is very much in love with him."

"No doubt; but it is not every man's fate to marry the woman who loves him best. Miss Hawkins perhaps wanted a home, and thought that this was the best offer she was likely to have."

"Yes," said Harriet, "and she might well think so, for no one could ever have a better. Well, I wish with all my heart that they may be happy."

Emma now felt sure that the worst of Harriet's trouble about Mr. Elton was over.

Thirty-six

MRS. ELTON

When the visit was returned, Emma had a better chance of forming an opinion about Mrs. Elton. Harriet happened not to be at Hartfield on that day. Mr. Woodhouse and Mr. Elton talked together, and during most of the visit Emma had Mrs. Elton to herself.

Emma soon made up her mind about Mrs. Elton. "She is a foolish woman," Emma thought, "very well-satisfied with herself, and thinking a great deal of her own importance. Her manners are bold and familiar. Except for the fact that she is rich, she will certainly not do Mr. Elton any good."

Mrs. Elton's sister was married to a rich man; and Mrs. Elton talked a great deal about the way in which this sister—Mrs. Suckling—lived. "Immediately I saw Hartfield," she said, "I thought how very much it is like my sister's place, Maple Grove. The grounds at Hartfield are, indeed, not so large as those at Maple Grove, but they are small and pretty; and in other ways the two places are so much alike, that I can assure you it is a great pleasure to me to be here. I spent so many happy days at Maple Grove! When you leave home, as I have done, Miss Woodhouse, you will understand how very delightful it is to meet with anything at all like what you have left behind."

Having pointed in this way to Emma's chance of being married, Mrs. Elton came a little nearer. She looked at Mr. Woodhouse and said, "Your father's health is far from good, I believe. He should go to Bath and drink the health waters there."

"My father went to Bath some years ago," said Emma, "but the waters did not do him any good. Dr. Perry does not think that it would be of any use for him to try them again."

"But Dr. Perry is probably wrong, Miss Woodhouse, as

country doctors so often are. It is quite wonderful how much good the Bath waters can do. I have seen it happen many times. And Bath is such a cheerful, happy place. That alone would help your father to forget his illness—for I suspect that he thinks about it more than he need. And for yourself, Miss Woodhouse, it is impossible to say what a visit to Bath might do. The usual results of a visit to Bath by a pretty young lady are very well known, I think."

Emma felt too angry to reply. With a look which was intended to be full of meaning, Mrs. Elton went on, "It is only too clear, Miss Woodhouse, that in Highbury you have very few chances—of the right kind. But in Bath everything would be very different. And I could at once make you known to the best people in the place. A letter from me to my friend, Mrs. Partridge, would at once bring you all the friends that you could wish for."

This was almost more than Emma felt that she could bear. She decided that she must change the subject of their talk.

"It would be quite impossible for us to go to Bath; and after all, Mrs. Elton, there are many interesting activities in Highbury. You are musical, I believe?"

"Yes, indeed," said Mrs. Elton. "Not that I am a good performer. I should not think of making such a claim. But I love music very much. I cannot do without it; it is a necessary of life to me. And when Mr. E. was speaking to me about my future home—when he told me how small his house is as compared with what I am used to, both in Bath and at Maple Grove, I replied, 'My dear, do not say another word. You have told me that the people of Highbury are musical, and that is enough. I can do without a large house, and with far fewer servants than I am accustomed to, but without music I cannot live'."

"I hope that Mr. Elton has not given you too high an idea of our music. After all, it will be very natural if he has."

"No, I am sure that he has not. For I have heard a great deal about you all since I came to Highbury; and I have heard, Miss Woodhouse, how delightfully you play. You and I must start a musical club, and have regular weekly meetings, at your house and mine. Something of the kind will be necessary for me; for without it I should not keep up my practice; a married woman, you know, has so many things to do."

"But, Mrs. Elton, you are so fond of music that you could not possibly let it go."

Mrs. Elton seemed quite doubtful on the point; but, after a moment's pause, she chose another subject.

"We have been visiting at Randalls," she said, "and found Mr. and Mrs. Weston both at home. They seem to be very pleasant people. I like them very much. *He* is a delightful man—quite a favourite with me already. And *she* appears so truly good, so motherly and kind-hearted. She was your governess, I think?"

Emma was almost too surprised to answer, but before she could do so Mrs. Elton went on—

"When I learnt that she was once a governess I was surprised to find her so very ladylike. But she is really quite a gentlewoman."

"Mrs. Weston's manners," said Emma, "were always good. She would be an example for any young woman."

"And who do you think came in while we were there?"

Emma could not form any idea. Mrs. Elton appeared to be speaking of a familiar friend.

"Knightley!" she continued; "Knightley. It was so fortunate, for I was out when he came to visit us the other day, and as he is a particular friend of Mr. E., I, of course, wished very much to see him. And I must say that Mr. E. has no reason to be ashamed of his friend. He is quite a gentleman. I liked him very much."

Fortunately the visit now came to an end. Mrs. Elton said that it was quite time for them to be gone. She and her husband went away, and Emma was left alone with her father.

Mr. Woodhouse now decided that it was time for him to rest a little. He went to his own room, leaving Emma at last with the time to give way to her feelings about Mrs. Elton.

"What a dreadful woman!" she thought. "Worse even than I supposed. Quite unbearable! 'Knightley!'—I could not have believed it. She never in her life saw him before, and she calls him Knightley; and she discovers that he is a gentleman! Certainly no one could call her a lady. An ill-mannered little person, with her Mr. E. and her Maple Grove and her friends at Bath and all her silly talk. And to think that she and I should unite to form a musical club—as if we were old friends. And Mrs. Weston!—that she should feel surprise at finding that the person who brought me up is a gentlewoman! Worse and worse. I never met with anyone like her. And to think that Mr. Elton chose her in preference to Harriet! Harriet is so much better than she is that one cannot think of them together. Oh! What would Frank Churchill say to her if he were here? What fun he would make of her! But there I am again—always thinking of Frank Churchill. How I catch myself out!"

Thirty-seven

MRS. ELTON AND JANE FAIRFAX

Emma took no notice of Mrs. Elton's idea that they should join together in forming a musical club. Mrs. Elton did not like this, and her manner towards Emma became cold and unfriendly. Emma also noticed that both Mr. and Mrs. Elton treated Harriet unkindly, and even rudely. "It is plain enough," Emma thought, "that he has told her the whole story about Harriet. They make fun of her, and also of me. It is painful; but it will certainly have one good result. Harriet's love for him cannot continue when she sees how he is treating her."

Miss Bates thought well of everybody, and it was not surprising, therefore, that she thought well of Mrs. Elton. And she had more reason for doing this because Mrs. Elton took a particular interest in Jane Fairfax.

One morning, soon after the Eltons' first visit to Hartfield, Emma met Mrs. Elton in the village.

"I have been visiting Mrs. and Miss Bates," said Mrs. Elton, "—such dear people, I am already quite fond of them, and I have been hearing Jane Fairfax play. Jane Fairfax is quite charming, Miss Woodhouse—a sweet, interesting creature. So quiet and ladylike; and how beautifully she plays the piano! I have enough knowledge of music to be able to be quite sure that Jane Fairfax plays very well indeed. And she is such a delightful person! You will laugh at my warmth, Miss Woodhouse, but I can talk of nothing but Jane Fairfax. And her place in life is so interesting, yet so sad. We must do something about it, Miss Woodhouse. We must bring her out. Such gifts as hers must not be allowed to remain unknown. I expect you have heard those charming lines of the poet—

> *'Full many a flower is born to blush unseen,*
> *And waste its fragrance on the desert air.'* *

We must not allow our dear Jane Fairfax to become an example of this."

"I do not think that Miss Fairfax has suffered in this way," said Emma. "You will understand this better when you know more about her. She has lived for many years with Colonel and Mrs. Campbell and she was educated with their daughter, who is her great friend. I am sure that her gifts were warmly recognised by the family—and by their friends."

"Ah, but she is now in such retirement, so thrown away. Whatever chances she may have had with the Campbells are now so plainly at an end. And I think she feels it. I am sure she does. She is quiet and silent. It is plain that she needs encouragement. I like her the better for it. I must confess that it is a recommendation to me. Jane Fairfax is a delightful character; she interests me more than I can say."

* Many flowers grow where no one can see them;
  Their smell is wasted where no one can smell them.

"She is not an easy person to help," said Emma. "You will find this, I think, when you have known her longer."

"Oh, but my dear Miss Woodhouse, a great deal can be done by those who dare to act. You and I need not be afraid. If we lead, others will follow; we can do what others cannot do. We have our carriages to fetch her and take her home. I shall certainly have Jane Fairfax very often at my house, and I shall have musical parties, so that people may know how gifted she is. And I shall be always looking for a good place for her as a governess. I shall make her known, of course, to my brother and sister, Mr. and Mrs. Suckling, when they come to us; for among the friends whom they see at Maple Grove there will certainly be someone who will be delighted to find such a governess as Jane Fairfax."

"Poor Jane Fairfax," Emma thought. "You have not deserved this. You may have done wrong in allowing the attentions of Mr. Dixon, and in accepting a piano which almost certainly comes from him; but this is too great a punishment even for that mistake."

This was the last talk of that kind that Emma had with Mrs. Elton. The change in Mrs. Elton's manner towards her appeared soon afterwards, and Emma was left in peace.

Thirty-eight

THE MYSTERY OF JANE FAIRFAX

When Mrs. Elton began to carry out the plans she had formed for helping Jane Fairfax, Miss Bates was very grateful. She thought that Mrs. Elton was a delightful woman—so kind, friendly and generous; so gifted and so well-educated. When Jane went out walking with Mrs. Elton, or when she spent whole days at her house, Miss Bates was delighted. She thought that the change would be so good for dear Jane; and she was very happy when she learned that Mrs. Elton was making enquiries among her wealthy friends about a place as governess for Jane.

One morning, Emma went to Randalls, and in the course of her visit she had a long talk with Mrs. Weston about Jane.

"I cannot understand," said Emma, "why Jane Fairfax stays in Highbury all this time, when she might be in Ireland with the Campbells."

"Well, Emma," said Mrs. Weston, "I think that Jane may have a reason for remaining in Highbury for a time. I know, indeed, that she has had very kind invitations both from the Campbells and the Dixons. Miss Bates told me that they not only asked her to come, but they promised to make all arrangements for the journey, even to the extent of sending servants to bring her over. But, as you see, she prefers to be here. Perhaps there is someone here whom she wishes to be near."

"Mrs. Weston," said Emma, with a smile, "you are still thinking that Mr. Knightley is in love with Jane—and, I suppose, that Jane is in love with him. You really must get that idea out of your head. As I have told you before, you are a very bad match-maker."

"Well, Emma, you may be right. I am not your equal in the business of match-making; but what other reason can there be? You cannot suppose that she prefers the company of her aunt and grandmother, and of the Eltons, to that of the Campbells and the Dixons."

The mention of the Dixons made Emma pause before replying.

"Jane Fairfax is a mystery," she said at last, "a complete mystery. Perhaps something is keeping her here—or at least keeping her from going to Ireland—which she cannot allow people to know. Perhaps she is ashamed of it."

Before Mrs. Weston could reply, Mr. George Knightley came in.

"We have been talking of Jane Fairfax," said Emma, "and wondering—among other things—how she can possibly bear to be so much in the company of Mrs. Elton."

"Well, Emma," said Mr. Knightley, "you must remember that Mrs. Elton probably behaves better to Jane Fairfax than she does to other people. Jane is so much above her in education, in manners, and in every other way, that Mrs. Elton cannot fail to see it. Although Mrs. Elton thinks so well of herself, she may not feel this in the presence of Jane Fairfax, for she may never have met a woman like her before."

"I know how highly you think of Jane Fairfax," said Emma. She was a little frightened by his warm praise of Jane.

"Yes," he replied, "anybody may know how highly I think of her."

"And yet," said Emma—thinking it was better to know the worst at once—"perhaps you may not yourself know *how* highly you think of her. You may be taken by surprise some day."

Mr. Knightley was certainly very much surprised at that moment. He gave Emma a strange and earnest look—a look of a kind which she remembered that he had sometimes given her before.

"No, Emma," he said, "you are quite mistaken. Jane Fairfax would probably not marry me, even if I asked her; and most certainly I shall never ask her."

"You do not think too highly of yourself, Mr. Knightley," said Emma, "I will say that for you."

"Well, Emma," he replied, "as you know, I admire Jane Fairfax, and I am sorry for her, but I have never once thought of her in the way you suspect. Now, Mrs. Weston, I must be going. Perhaps, Emma, you will give me the pleasure of allowing me to walk back to Hartfield with you."

Thirty-nine

A DINNER PARTY AT HARTFIELD

Everybody in or near Highbury who had ever visited Mr. Elton before he was married, now came to pay a marriage visit to him and his bride. Dinner parties and evening parties were made for them both, and Mrs. Elton soon found that it was only very seldom that she had a free evening.

"I see how it is," she said. "I see what a life I am to lead among you. We really seem to be quite famous. If this is living in the country, it is hardly more quiet than living in a town. From next Monday to Saturday we are going out to a party every day."

Emma felt that in spite of her dislike of Mrs. Elton she must not do less than other people were doing. Her father with some hesitation agreed that they must give a dinner party, and, now that this was settled, it was not difficult to decide who should be invited to it. Besides the Eltons, they must ask the Westons, Mr. George Knightley and Jane Fairfax.

When Emma had arranged to have dinner for eight people —including herself and her father—a rather unfortunate difficulty arose. Some months ago, Mr. John Knightley promised that he would soon bring his two eldest boys to spend some weeks at Hartfield with Mr. Woodhouse and Emma; and the day on which he now decided to bring them was the very day of the dinner party. He could only stay one night at Hartfield and his business would not allow him to come on any other day. Emma and her father were both sorry when John Knightley's letter arrived. Mr. Woodhouse felt that eight people at dinner were quite as many as he could bear; and Emma was sure that John Knightley, who would be the ninth member of her party, would be in a bad temper. He expected that, when he brought his boys to Hartfield, he would spend a quiet evening there with his brother and with Emma and her father. He would think it hard that, on the one evening he could be at Hartfield, he should find a dinner party there.

It happened that on the day of the party Mr. Weston was suddenly called to London on business. He wrote, "I am very sorry indeed that I cannot have the pleasure of coming with Mrs. Weston to dinner at Hartfield, but I shall hope to be with you later in the evening." Emma was very glad to find that there would now be only eight people at dinner; and, when John Knightley arrived with his two boys, she was also glad to find that he was in a good temper. He did not seem to dislike the dinner party as much as she feared that he would. He behaved very well at dinner, and when Emma went, with the other ladies, to the sitting-room, she felt that, so far, the evening had passed off well.

In the sitting-room Mrs. Elton succeeded in keeping Jane Fairfax almost entirely to herself, so that it was necessary for Emma and Mrs. Weston either to talk to one another or to be silent. Mrs. Elton sometimes spoke to Jane in a half-whisper, but in spite of this ill-mannered attempt to make a secret of what she was saying, Emma and Mrs. Weston could hardly help hearing it. It was clear that she was talking to Jane about her chances of obtaining a place as governess.

"Here is April come!" said Mrs. Elton. "I get quite anxious about you. June will soon be here."

"But I have never fixed on June or any other month; I merely thought that, sometime this summer——"

"But have you really heard of nothing?"

"I have made no attempt to hear of anything. I do not wish to do so at present."

"Oh, but my dear Jane, we cannot begin too early. You cannot know how difficult it is to get places of this kind."

"Cannot know it!" said Jane, with a rather unhappy smile, "Dear Mrs. Elton, who can have thought about it as I have done?"

"But you have not seen so much of the world as I have. You do not know how many well-educated young women there are who are always seeking the best places. I have seen so much of this at Maple Grove. Now a friend of Mrs. Suckling's, Mrs. Bragge, who is very rich, will soon want a governess. You would be surprised at the number of letters on the subject she has already received. A great many young women—some of them less well qualified than you are—wished to be in her family. And, indeed, of all houses in the land, this is the one which I most wish to see you in."

"I must ask you not to do anything about it at present," said Jane. "Colonel and Mrs. Campbell are to be in London again in July, and they will wish me to spend some time with

them. Until then, I do not wish you to take the trouble of making any enquiries for me."

"Trouble! You are afraid of giving me trouble," exclaimed Mrs. Elton. "I assure you, my dear Jane, the Campbells cannot be more interested in you than I am. I shall write to Mrs. Partridge in a day or two, and ask her to look for a place that would suit you."

In this way Mrs. Elton ran on. Nothing that Jane said could stop her, but at last Mr. Woodhouse entered the room. "Here comes this dear old friend of mine," Mrs. Elton whispered. "How kind it is of him to come before the other men. What a dear creature he is! I wish you could have heard his polite speeches to me at dinner. I think I must be rather a favourite. He noticed my dress. I do hope that I am not over-dressed; but a bride, you know, must appear like a bride."

The other men now followed Mr. Woodhouse to the sitting-room, and among them came Mr. Weston. He had returned from London to a late dinner at Randalls, and had walked to Hartfield after it was over. Mr. Woodhouse was almost as glad to see him now as he would have been sorry to see him before. All the others had expected him. Only John Knightley was surprised. That a man who might have spent his evening quietly at home after a day of business in London, should choose to set off again, and walk nearly a mile to another man's house, was more than he could understand. "I could not have believed it," he said.

Forty

MR. WESTON BRINGS GOOD NEWS

The first thing that Mr. Weston did when he entered the sitting-room was to hand a letter to Mrs. Weston. It was addressed to her, but Mr. Weston had opened it. It was from Frank.

"Read it, read it," he said. "It will give you pleasure. Only a few lines. It will not take you long. Read it to Emma."

The two ladies looked over it together; he sat smiling and talking to them the whole time.

"Well, he is coming, you see; good news, I think. What do you say to it? I always said that he would be here again before long. The Churchills are coming to London for a time, and while they are there, Frank will often be able to come and see us. This is exactly what I wanted. We could not have better news."

It was clear that Mrs. Weston was very pleased with her letter. The news that Frank would soon be at Randalls again made her very happy. Emma could not be so sure about her own feelings; but although she could not describe them to herself, she knew that she was feeling a great deal.

Mr. Weston now went round the room, telling his good news to the other guests. He was so full of it himself, and it gave him so much pleasure, that he did not notice its effect upon others. Otherwise he might have seen that the news did not appear to be very welcome either to Mr. Woodhouse or to Mr. George Knightley. Mr. Knightley, indeed, found it difficult not to show how much he disliked Frank Churchill, and how sorry he was to hear that Frank would soon be at Randalls again.

Mr. Weston now came to Mrs. Elton, the one person in the room to whom Frank was not already known.

"I hope I shall soon have the pleasure of making my son known to you," he said. "You have no doubt heard of Frank Churchill, and you know that he is my son, although he has a different name."

"Oh, yes," said Mrs. Elton, "I have indeed heard of him and I shall be very happy to meet him. I am sure that Mr. Elton will lose no time in visiting him, and we shall both have great pleasure in seeing him at our house."

"You are very kind," said Mr. Weston. "Frank will be here quite soon. We had the news in a letter which came this morning. I met the postman after I left the house. It was addressed to Mrs. Weston, as all Frank's letters are. It is only very seldom that he writes to me. But I was so anxious to hear the news that I opened the letter—and I found that it brought very good news."

"Oh, Mr. Weston," said Mrs. Elton, "how can you tell me that you opened a letter that was addressed to your wife? I cannot agree with this. It is a most dangerous practice, and I hope that none of your neighbours will follow your example. If this is what we are to expect, we married women must begin to take care of ourselves. Oh, Mr. Weston, I could not have believed it of you!"

"Yes, we men are sad fellows. You must learn to take care of yourself, Mrs. Elton. The letter I opened was a short letter, written in a hurry. It tells us that they are all coming to London because of Mrs. Churchill's health. She has not been well this winter and she thinks that Enscombe is too cold for her; so they are moving to their London house without loss of time. It is a long journey—about 190 miles."

"Yes, a long journey, indeed—sixty-five miles longer than the journey from Maple Grove—my brother's place—to London. But, Mr. Weston, what is distance to wealthy people? You will hardly believe it, but twice in one week my brother, Mr. Suckling, with his friend, Mr. Bragge, went to London and back again with four horses."

Mr. Weston showed suitable surprise. "Frank's letter," he went on, "tells us that his aunt, Mrs. Churchill, has been too weak to move from one room to another without the support of both his arm and his uncle's. This, as you see, shows great weakness. Yet she is now so anxious to be in London that she means to sleep only two nights upon the road. Weak ladies, Mrs. Elton, can sometimes show that they are very strong—when they wish it. You must agree with me in that."

"No, indeed, I shall agree to nothing. I am a woman, and I shall always take the woman's side."

"Well, Mrs. Elton, you have perhaps noticed already that I am not particularly fond of Mrs. Churchill. You may have heard that Frank was here for two weeks in February. We arranged a dance at the Crown, but, most unfortunately, Mrs. Churchill was ill—or thought she was ill—and Frank was called home before the dance could be held."

"Yes, I have heard of it," said Mrs. Elton. "Indeed, I expect I have heard a great deal more of Mr. Frank Churchill than he has heard of me."

"My dear Madam," said Mr. Weston, "nobody but yourself could imagine such a thing possible. Not heard of you! Why, I believe that, since you arrived, Mrs. Weston's letters to Frank have been full of very little else than Mrs. Elton."

The talk was now stopped, for coffee was brought in, and Mrs. Elton was claimed by Mr. Woodhouse who wished to show proper attention to the bride.

Forty-one

AUNT EMMA AND UNCLE GEORGE

After the coffee Mr. and Mrs. Weston and Mr. Elton sat down with Mr. Woodhouse to play cards. The remaining five were left to amuse one another, and Emma did not find that they succeeded in doing so very well. Jane Fairfax clearly had no intention of listening to anything more that Mrs. Elton might have to say about obtaining a place for her in a wealthy family. She appeared, indeed, to be lost in thought. Mr. George Knightley was equally silent. He looked like a man who has received unwelcome news. He occasionally said a few words to Jane Fairfax and she replied rather sadly, but they soon became silent again. Mrs. Elton seemed to be wanting to be noticed, but neither of the Mr. Knightleys would do anything to help her. To Emma's surprise, it was Mr. John Knightley who was the most willing to talk. He was to leave early on the next day and he soon began with—

"Well, Emma, I do not think that I have anything more to

say to you about the boys. Isabella has written you a long letter, and everything is down at full length there, we may be sure. All that I can add to it—and this may, perhaps, not quite agree with what Isabella has said—is—'Do not spoil them and do not give them any medicine'."

"I hope that I shall satisfy you both," said Emma, "for I shall do all that I can to make them happy, which will be enough for Isabella; and if they are happy, they will not need either to be spoiled or to be given medicine."

"And if you find them troublesome you must send them home again."

"Do you really think that the boys are going to give me any trouble? And even if they do, do you think that I shall send them home?"

"Well, Emma, I think it possible that they may be too noisy for your father—for boys cannot help being boys, you know. And as to yourself, you seem to go to so many more parties than you used to do, and you see so many more people at Hartfield, that I cannot help fearing that you will find the boys rather troublesome."

"More parties!" said Emma, "more visitors at Hartfield! What can you possibly mean?"

"Surely, Emma, you must agree that the last half-year has made a great difference to your way of life."

"Difference! No, indeed, I do not."

"But, Emma, here am I, come down from London for only one day, and I find that you and your father have a dinner party. When did it happen before? Or anything like it? A little while ago, every letter to Isabella brought an account of fresh parties—dinners at the Coles, or dances at the Crown. The difference which Randalls alone makes to your life is very great."

"Yes," said his brother, "it is Randalls that does it all."

"Very well," said John Knightley; "and there will be no change, I suppose in Randalls; so it seems to me quite likely that the two boys will sometimes be in the way. If they are, you must send them home."

"No," said his brother. "It is quite unnecessary to do that. Send them to Donwell Abbey. I shall have plenty of time for them."

Emma looked at George Knightley and laughed. "You amuse me," she said. "You know very well that when I go to a party you are always there yourself. We do not go to very many—as your brother thinks—but when one of us is busy in this way, the other is too. If I am supposed to have no time for taking care of little boys, you are just as badly off. But what, in fact, are all these parties to which we are supposed to go? A dinner party at the Coles, and a dance at the Crown which never happened. You, Mr. John Knightley, are no doubt very fortunate in meeting so many old friends, and in coming to know Mrs. Elton, on the day on which you happen to come to visit us; but your brother will tell you how very seldom I am ever away from Hartfield for more than two hours at a time. And as for the dear little boys, I must say that if Aunt Emma has not time for them, I do not think that Uncle George will find more time, or even so much; for he is away from home a great deal more often than Aunt Emma, and when he is there, he is either reading or settling his accounts."

Mr. George Knightley seemed to be trying not to smile, and he succeeded without difficulty when Mrs. Elton began to talk to him.

Forty-two

THE DANCE AT THE CROWN

The next letter which Mrs. Weston received from Frank Churchill contained even better news. His uncle and aunt had decided to leave London for two months, and they had taken a house with furniture in it at Richmond—only nine miles from Highbury. Frank wrote in the highest spirits and Mr. Weston was delighted. "For two months," he said, "Frank will be quite near us. He will always be coming over; for what are nine miles to a young man?—an hour's ride."

Emma felt that she must now think seriously about herself and Frank. "Am I in love with him?" she asked herself. "Perhaps at one time I was—just a little. But I do not think I am now; for if I were, I should not have been so pleased when, in a letter to Mrs. Weston, he referred with so much feeling to my beautiful little friend. Is he still in love with me? for when he left Highbury I think that he certainly was; indeed, he *almost* told me so. I must be very careful not to let that happen again, for it would completely spoil our friendship —and I value his friendship very much. It would be sad indeed if I were to lose it."

It was not long before Frank rode down to Randalls for a few hours, and from there he went on to Hartfield. He and Emma met with perfect friendliness. Emma had no doubt that he was pleased to see her; but she also felt an instant doubt as to whether he cared for her as much as he had once done. She watched him carefully, and she was quite sure that he was not as much in love with her as he was when he went away. Absence, and probably also a suspicion that she did not return his love, had produced this very natural and desirable result.

The dance now took place at the Crown. Nothing happened to prevent it, and all the arrangements made for three months ago were now successfully carried out—all the arrangements except one; for Frank and Emma did not lead the dance.

When Emma arrived at the Crown, Frank came to her immediately and asked her to remember her former promise; but, at that moment, Mr. and Mrs. Weston came to them, both with a slightly troubled look.

"Frank," said Mr. Weston, "there is a little difficulty. Mrs. Elton must be asked to lead the dance. She will expect it, you know."

"But," said Frank, "the first two dances were promised to

me by Miss Woodhouse three months ago—before we ever heard of Mrs. Elton."

"Well, Frank," said Mrs. Weston, "I have no doubt that Mrs. Elton will think that you ought to ask her; but in any case, as the bride, she must lead the dance. Perhaps your father will ask her?"

Mrs. Weston looked at her husband and he at once did as she wished. He sought out Mrs. Elton, and when the music began, he led her into the dance. Frank and Emma followed. Emma found herself standing second to Mrs. Elton, although she had always understood that the dance was particularly for her. It was almost enough to make her think of marrying.

It was certainly a victory for Mrs. Elton. She intended to begin with Frank, but she could not lose in importance by dancing with his father—and she was at the top of the dance. Her self-importance was completely satisfied.

Emma did not allow this to prevent her own happiness. She looked down the long line of dancers and she felt that she had many hours of happiness before her. The only thing that troubled her was that Mr. George Knightley was not dancing. He was standing among the elderly men—the husbands and fathers, who were pretending to show an interest in the dancing until supper was ready. "George Knightley has no right to place himself among such people," Emma thought. "He does not belong to them. He looks so young that everyone must think as I do, that he ought to be dancing."

When he moved a few steps nearer to her, those few steps were enough to show how gracefully he would dance if he would only take the trouble. Whenever his eyes met hers, she forced him to smile, but at other times he looked serious. Emma knew that, through some strange want of sympathy, he did not like the young man with whom she was dancing. She wished that he could like Frank Churchill better, and above all she wished that he would dance.

Forty-three

NOT BROTHER AND SISTER

The last two dances before supper began, and Emma was surprised to notice that Harriet was not dancing. Until then, everyone who wished to dance had been able to do so, for the numbers of men and women were equal; but now Harriet was left out. Emma could not understand this until she happened to see Mr. Elton walking about. She knew that he would not ask Harriet to dance if it was possible not to do so, and she expected every moment to see him escape into the small room.

That, however, was not Mr. Elton's plan. He walked up and down the room, and he was sometimes quite close to Harriet, but he did not ask her to dance. Mrs. Weston soon left her seat and went up to Mr. Elton with a smile—

"Are you dancing, Mr. Elton?" she said.

"Most certainly, Mrs. Weston," he replied, "if you will dance with me."

"Oh, I am not dancing. I have too many things to see to. I must go to see when the supper will be ready. But Miss Smith is not dancing. Will you ask her?"

"Oh, I had not noticed; but I hope you will excuse me, Mrs. Weston. I am an old married man, and my dancing days are really over."

At that moment Emma noticed that Mr. Elton and his wife looked at one another, and that a smile of amusement passed between them. Mr. Elton then walked to where Mr. Knightley was standing and began talking to him. Mr. Knightley did not reply, however, but walked away, and the next moment Emma saw with delight and surprise that he was asking Harriet to dance.

Mr. Knightley's dancing proved to be just as she expected—extremely good. It was clear that Harriet was very happy.

Mr. Elton went out of the room, looking very foolish, Emma thought. She said to herself, "He is not yet as bad as his wife, although he is growing very like her." At that moment Emma heard Mrs. Elton say to the gentleman with whom she was dancing, "Knightley has taken pity on poor little Miss Smith. Very good-natured, I am sure."

Emma had no chance of speaking to George Knightley until after supper. She then thanked him very warmly for dancing with Harriet. He strongly blamed the Eltons for what they had done. "They aimed at wounding Harriet—and you also," he said. "Emma, why is it that they are your enemies?"

Emma did not reply. He looked at her with a smile and said, "Confess, Emma! You wanted Mr. Elton to marry Harriet."

"I did," she replied, "and they cannot forgive me."

"I will not blame you," he said. "I will leave you to your own thoughts."

"Can you safely leave me to them?" she asked. "My thoughts have so often been wrong. I can see now that I was completely mistaken about Mr. Elton. There is a littleness about him which you discovered, and I did not. And I really believed that he was in love with Harriet. It was a terrible mistake."

"And in return for your saying so much," he said, "I will myself say that you chose for him better than he chose for himself. Harriet Smith would have been a far better wife for him than the woman he married. Harriet is not only beautiful, but she is well-mannered and simple. She has been better educated than I thought, and she has greatly improved under your care. I enjoyed the talk I had with her."

They were now stopped by Mr. Weston, who was calling upon the young people to begin dancing again. "Come, Emma," he said, "set the others an example. Everybody is lazy. Everybody is asleep."

"I am ready, whenever I am wanted," said Emma.

"With whom are you going to dance?" asked George Knightley.

Emma hesitated a moment, and then replied, "With you, if you will ask me."

"Will you?" he said, offering his hand.

"Indeed, I will. You have shown that you can dance, and you know we are not really so much brother and sister as to make it at all improper."

"Brother and sister!—No, indeed!"

Forty-four

AN ADVENTURE WITH THE GIPSIES

On the morning after the dance, Emma was walking about the grass in front of the house at Hartfield, feeling very happy. She had many pleasant memories of the dance, but the one which gave her most pleasure was her talk with George Knightley about the Eltons. She was glad that he agreed with her so well on that subject, and his praise of Harriet was exactly what she wished to hear. It gave her the satisfaction of feeling that she had done a great deal for Harriet, although she had also made the sad mistake of encouraging her to fall in love with Mr. Elton. And she felt that the treatment which Harriet received last night from the Eltons would cure her finally of this love.

With Harriet cured, and Frank Churchill not too much in love with herself, and George Knightley no longer wishing to quarrel with her, Emma felt that she could look forward to being very happy this summer.

She was not to see Frank Churchill this morning. He had told her that he could not allow himself the pleasure of stopping at Hartfield, as he must be home by the middle of the day.

Having settled all these matters to her satisfaction, Emma turned towards the house, feeling that she was now quite ready to do all that was necessary for her father and the two little boys. But at that moment the iron gate at the end of the path which led up to the house was opened, and two persons

HARRIET'S ADVENTURE WITH THE GIPSIES

appeared whom Emma never less expected to see together—Harriet and Frank Churchill. Emma saw in a moment that something extraordinary had happened. Harriet was resting on Frank's arm. She looked white and frightened and he was trying to cheer her. When they reached the house, Harriet immediately sank into a chair and fainted away.

Emma sent a servant for the usual medicines, and when all that was possible had been done for Harriet, she listened to the story which Frank told her.

"You may be surprised to learn, Miss Woodhouse, that I did not set out on horseback this morning as I told you last night that I would. I saw that it would be a beautiful day, and I thought that, for a few miles, I would prefer to walk instead of hurrying through this lovely country. So I sent my servant on with our horses to an inn a few miles beyond Highbury where I could meet him later. Before starting on my walk, it was necessary for me to visit Miss Bates, in order to return a small knife which she kindly lent me last night. I was delayed there, but at last I set out, and I had not walked far along the Richmond Road when I saw, a little way off, what appeared to be a camp of gipsies. As I came nearer, I was surprised to see that some of the gipsies and their children had surrounded a young lady. She was very frightened and was crying for help; and I at once recognised her voice as the voice of Miss Smith."

"Good heavens! How did she come there?" said Emma, "and what did you do?"

"I learned later," said Frank, "that Miss Smith and Miss Beckerton set out from Mrs. Goddard's for a walk. When they came to the gipsies' camp some of the children begged money from them. Miss Smith opened her bag and gave them what she had, but they were soon demanding more. Miss Beckerton succeeded in getting away. Miss Smith tried to follow, but the gipsies stopped her, thinking no doubt that there was more money in her bag which they intended to have. Luckily, at this moment I arrived. It was not difficult to deal with the gipsies. They were soon quite as frightened as Miss Smith. I gave her my arm. We set out along the road, and fortunately Miss Smith was able to walk as far as the Hartfield gates. I very much hope that she will be none the worse for the adventure."

"We both owe you the most grateful thanks," said Emma. "What would have happened if you had not been there is too terrible to think of."

Harriet was now recovering, and her thanks were joined to Emma's. Frank said that he must go at once to the inn at which his servant was waiting for him with his horses.

"My uncle and aunt will be getting anxious," he said, "for I promised them that I would be at Richmond early in the day. I cannot, however, regret my delay, since it has enabled me to be of some small service to Miss Smith."

Emma and Harriet again expressed their warmest thanks. He replied, with a happy smile, that it was "only what any man would have done," and in a few moments he was gone.

Emma now told Harriet to go and lie down; she sent a servant to tell Mrs. Goddard that Harriet was safe at Hartfield; she told her father of Harriet's adventure, and did her best to calm his fears when he learned that there was a gipsy camp near Highbury; and she gave some necessary orders to servants about her two little nephews. When she had done all these things, Emma at last had time to think.

"Could anything be more extraordinary," she said to herself, "than that such a thing as this should happen, just at this time, to Frank and to Harriet? Frank, I suspect, has been doing his best to overcome his love for me—since I have shown him plainly that I do not love him in the way he wishes; and Harriet is just recovering from her love for Mr. Elton. And now these two young people are brought together in a way which cannot fail to make them extremely interested in one another."

Emma thought about it for a long time. At last she said to herself, "I am not going to interfere. I have had enough of interference, and I know what terrible mistakes it is possible to make. But, quite a long time ago, Frank wrote to Mrs. Weston about my 'beautiful little friend', and now he has saved her from great danger. If things turn out as I wish, this will have been a happy day for Harriet."

Forty-five

HARRIET DECIDES THAT SHE WILL NEVER MARRY

The story of the gipsies caused great excitement in Highbury. The dance at the Crown was forgotten, and Harriet's adventure took its place as the subject people talked about. Miss Beckerton was blamed for deserting Harriet, but she explained that she thought that Harriet was following her, and that when she found that this was not so, she ran on to look for help and to warn the neighbourhood. Frank Churchill was warmly praised. He certainly frightened the gipsies, for they took themselves off in a hurry, and it became known that the young ladies of Highbury might go for country walks with as much safety as before. The story was soon forgotten except by Emma's two little nephews. They asked to have it told to them again and again, and if Emma made the smallest change in the story as she told it first, they immediately put her right.

One morning when Harriet was at Hartfield, she and Emma were talking about the dance. It was clear that, as Emma expected, the behaviour of the Eltons had made a great difference to Harriet.

"Dear Miss Woodhouse," she said, "I am ashamed of giving way as I have done. I can see nothing at all extraordinary in him now. I do not care whether I meet him or not, except that, of the two, I would rather not meet him; and, indeed, I would go a long way round not to meet him."

"I am very glad to hear you say so, Harriet," said Emma. "He and his wife certainly treated you very unkindly at the dance."

"Yes," said Harriet, "I felt it deeply. I could not have believed it of either of them. I no longer admire his wife as I have done. No doubt she is very charming, but I think her very unkind and ill-mannered. I shall never forget her look the other night."

"Yes, Harriet. I saw it, and I was deeply sorry for it, though it did not surprise me. But you had your dance before supper after all."

Harriet blushed. "Yes," she said, "and I shall never forget that either."

"Mr. Elton looked very foolish."

"Well, Miss Woodhouse, I do not wish either of them any harm. Let them be as happy together as they can. As for myself, I know now that I shall never marry."

Emma looked at Harriet with some surprise.

"Never marry, Harriet! What can be the cause of this? You have, I know, been very unhappy; and it grieves me to remember that I was partly to blame for this. Are you quite sure that you are not still unhappy about Mr. Elton?"

"Mr. Elton!" cried Harriet. "Oh, Miss Woodhouse, how could you possibly think of such a thing?"

Emma then remembered that almost the last time Harriet came to Hartfield, she was in a fainting condition and leaning on Frank Churchill's arm.

"Then what reason can you possibly have for deciding never to marry?"

Harriet hesitated. At last she almost whispered, "If one meets with someone so much above one—and if he——"

"Harriet," said Emma, "I cannot pretend not to understand you. Your reason for thinking that you will not marry is that you love someone whom you think that you could never marry, because he is of a class above your own. I respect you for it, and when I remember what he did for you——"

"Oh, Miss Woodhouse, how can I possibly forget it? But, of course, I am not so foolish as to think it possible—I can only admire him from a distance."

"Well, Harriet," said Emma, "of course, I can see that your feelings are very natural, and I do not advise you to give way to them. I cannot promise that they will be returned. But more unlikely things have happened. We have mentioned no names, and henceforward I know nothing of the matter. I have decided that in future I will do nothing either to help people to fall in love or to prevent them from doing so."

Harriet took Emma's hand and kissed it silently and gratefully. Emma thought, "It will not do Harriet any harm to be in love with Frank Churchill for a time, even if he does not return her love. He is a gentleman—very different from Mr. Martin—and Harriet's interest in him will raise and educate her mind."

Forty-six

MRS. ELTON AND MR. KNIGHTLEY

After being long fed with hopes of an early visit from Mr. and Mrs. Suckling of Maple Grove, the people of Highbury were sorry to learn that they could not possibly come until the autumn. Mrs. Elton was more sorry than anybody. For her it was the delay of a great deal of pleasure and pride. Mrs. Elton intended, with the help of the Sucklings and their two carriages, to arrange parties of her friends to visit Box Hill and other places of interest or beauty. At first she thought that these parties must be put off, but she decided that she and her friends might at least spend a day on Box Hill.

It was now the middle of June and the weather was fine. Mrs. Elton was impatient to fix the day of the party, but just at this time an accident happened to one of Mr. Elton's carriage horses, and it was quite uncertain how long it would be before the horse could be used.

"How sad this is, Knightley!" said Mrs. Elton one day to the owner of Donwell Abbey when he was visiting her husband. "What are we to do? We have arranged a most delightful party for Box Hill, and it is quite uncertain when we shall be able to go."

"You had better come to Donwell Abbey," he replied. "You can get there without horses. Come and eat my strawberries*; they are ripening fast."

If Mr. Knightley did not say this seriously, he soon found that there was no escape. His invitation was accepted with delight by Mrs. Elton on behalf of herself and her husband. She was a little uncertain at the moment as to how much further she might go.

"You may depend upon us," she said. "Name your day and we will come. May I ask Jane Fairfax to come?"

* Strawberry—a very nice small red fruit which grows on the ground.

"I cannot name a day," he said, "until I have spoken to some others whom I should wish to meet you."

"Oh, leave it all to me!" cried Mrs. Elton. "It is my party, you know. I will bring with me the friends who would have come to Box Hill."

"I hope you will bring Elton," he replied, "but I think it will be best for me to send the other invitations myself."

"Ah, but you need not be afraid, Knightley. I am a married woman, you know, and you are quite safe. It is my party. Leave it all to me, and I will invite your guests."

"Mrs. Elton," he replied, "there is only one married woman whom I can allow to invite guests to Donwall, and that is——"

"Mrs. Weston, I suppose," said Mrs. Elton, with a rather disappointed look.

"No—Mrs. George Knightley, and until there is such a person I prefer to send such invitations myself."

"Ah, you are an odd creature," said Mrs. Elton—satisfied to have no one preferred to herself. "Well, I shall bring Jane with me—Jane and her aunt. The rest I leave to you. Perhaps you may wish to know that I am quite willing to meet the Hartfield family. They are friends of yours, I know."

"You will certainly meet them if they can come. And as to Miss Bates and Miss Fairfax, I will go and see them on my way home."

Forty-seven

DONWELL ABBEY

The strawberry beds at Donwell Abbey were famous, and Mr. Knightley's friends were very willing to come and visit them. Emma was glad to know that the visit to Box Hill was put off; and she was pleased with the idea of spending a morning at Donwell Abbey. Her father made no difficulty about going, if the weather was fine. He had not been to Donwell for two years. "I shall like to see it again," he said. "You tell me that the Westons are going. I am sure that poor Miss Taylor will sit with me indoors, while the young people gather strawberries and walk about the gardens."

When Mr. Knightley went to Randalls to invite the Westons, Mr. Weston, without being asked, said that he would get Frank to join them, if possible. Mr. Knightley had to say that he would be glad to see Frank; but a few days later he was still more glad to learn that Frank would probably not be able to come, for Mrs. Churchill was now seriously ill.

When the day came, the sun was shining, and the house and gardens at Donwell Abbey looked very beautiful. Mr. Woodhouse was soon comfortably settled with Mrs. Weston, and Emma went out for a walk in the Abbey grounds. She was in no hurry to join the other members of the party. It gave her pleasure to see once more the surroundings of this beautiful old house, and to remember that her own family was closely related to the owner of it.

"Isabella has married well," she thought. "John Knightley has some faults of temper, but he is a good man—a good husband and a good father. The family of the Knightleys is old and respectable. They have been the owners of Donwell Abbey for hundreds of years. I am proud to be related to them.'

Emma was now at the end of the Abbey grounds, near the river. Across the river was the Abbey-Mill Farm. It was a sweet view, and two people were standing looking at it— Mr. Knightley and Harriet. Emma was glad to see them together. There was a time when Mr. Knightley would have disliked Harriet as a companion, but now he seemed to be having a pleasant talk with her.

"Not very long ago," Emma thought, "I should have been sorry to see Harriet looking across at Abbey-Mill Farm, where, only last summer, she spent so many happy weeks in company with the Martins; but Robert Martin no longer has a dangerous place in Harriet's thoughts. It is of Frank Churchill that she

EMMA SEES MR. KNIGHTLEY AND HARRIET BY THE RIVER

is thinking now. We have agreed to mention no names, and we have both kept to the agreement; but Harriet is a simple-minded girl, and it is not difficult to read her thoughts."

Mr. Knightley now called the party together and asked them to come into the house for some refreshments. Before the meal was over, a message came from Frank Churchill saying that his aunt was dead, and that he could not come to Donwell Abbey.

Harriet appeared to bear this news very well. "She certainly has more strength of character than she used to have," Emma thought.

Forty-eight

A SECRET IS OUT

One morning, about ten days after the visit to Donwell Abbey, Mr. Weston came to Hartfield and asked to see Emma immediately. "Can you come to Randalls this morning?" he said. "Mrs. Weston wishes to see you. Indeed, she *must* see you."

"Good heavens!" said Emma, "what is the matter? Is Mrs. Weston ill?"

"No, she is not ill—but something extraordinary has happened. Do not ask me what it is, but come with me at once to Randalls. I promised my wife that she should break the news to you herself."

"Break it to me! Mr. Weston, please tell me immediately. It is cruel to keep me waiting. Someone is ill; someone is dead. I must know at once who it is."

"No one is ill," he replied, "and only Mrs. Churchill is dead; but you know that already. Frank has been with us this morning. He is now on his way home again."

"The news is about Frank?"

"Do not ask me, Emma. Remember my promise to Mrs. Weston."

When they arrived at Randalls, Emma saw that Mrs. Weston looked very ill.

"What is it, my dear friend?" Emma asked, "something very unpleasant has happened, I find. Please tell me what it is."

"Can you not guess, Emma? Have you no idea of what you are to hear?"

"All that I can guess," said Emma, "is that, in some way that I do not yet understand, the news is about Mr. Frank Churchill."

"You are right, Emma. Frank has been here this morning; and he has told us something which has made us both very unhappy—and we fear that you will be unhappy too."

"But what is it?"

"He has fallen in love. Indeed, he has been long in love, and he has promised to marry——"

"But whom?"

"You will scarcely believe it—Jane Fairfax!"

Emma was almost too surprised to answer. "Jane Fairfax!" she said at last, "but how is this possible? I cannot understand it. When did it begin?"

"It began at Weymouth last October," said Mrs. Weston, "before either of them came to Highbury. They told no one—neither the Campbells, nor her family, nor his. As you know, Emma, when Frank came to visit us, we had not the slightest idea that he had made this promise of marriage. We believed that he was completely free—and he acted as if he was free. For this part of his behaviour we feel that he is seriously to blame. It was very wrong; and if, Emma——"

Mrs. Weston hesitated. She looked anxiously at Emma.

"Mrs. Weston," said Emma, "I will not pretend that I do not understand you. But I can at once remove any anxiety that you may be feeling for me. I will confess that, when I knew Mr. Churchill first, I was inclined to be a little in love with him—and I must say that I had some good reasons for thinking that he was in love with me. Like you, I feel that his behaviour was very wrong. But, fortunately for me, the feeling which I once had for him did not last. For three months at least, I have cared nothing for him. You may believe me, Mrs. Weston; this is the simple truth."

Mrs. Weston kissed her with tears of joy.

"Mr. Weston will be quite as glad as I am," she said. "You must have known, my dear Emma, how much we both hoped that you and Frank would become interested in one another; and we thought that it was so. Imagine, then, what we have been feeling on your account."

"I have escaped," said Emma, "but this does not excuse him, Mrs. Weston, nor does it excuse Jane Fairfax. They have been very wrong, to come among us, as they have done, with this secret between themselves. And why do they tell us now?"

"While Mrs. Churchill was alive, Frank knew that he must keep his secret. But he has now told Mr. Churchill, who is an easy man to deal with; and, in his way, he is fond of Frank. He agreed to the marriage without much difficulty."

"Ah!" thought Emma, "he would have done as much for Harriet."

For that was now the thought which most filled her mind— that, and also the memory of her suspicions about Mr. Dixon, and her talk on that subject with Frank Churchill. "He deceived us all," she said to herself. "I can never forgive him. And Harriet! Poor Harriet!"

Forty-nine

EMMA AND HARRIET

The Westons asked Emma to say nothing about the news they had told her. For the present it was to remain a secret. But, as Emma was soon to learn, Mr. Weston was not good at keeping secrets.

A few mornings later, Harriet came to Hartfield. She entered the sitting-room very cheerfully, and said to Emma, "Well, Miss Woodhouse, is not this the oddest news that ever was?"

"What news?" asked Emma.

"About Jane Fairfax. Did you ever hear of anything so strange? I met Mr. Weston just now, and he told it to me as a great secret. He said that I was not to mention it to anybody but you, but that you knew it already."

"What did Mr. Weston tell you?"

"Oh, he told me all about it; that Jane Fairfax and Mr. Frank Churchill are engaged* to be married and that they

* Are engaged—have promised to marry.

have been secretly engaged to one another for a long time. How very odd!"

Harriet's behaviour was, indeed, so odd that Emma could not understand it. Her character seemed to be quite changed. Emma looked at her, unable to speak.

"Had you no idea," said Harriet, "that he was in love with her? I thought perhaps you might—you, who can see into everybody's heart."

"Harriet," said Emma, "I do not understand you, and I begin to doubt very much whether I am able to look into people's hearts. Can you seriously ask me whether I thought that Mr. Churchill was in love with Jane Fairfax, when I was at least not trying to stop what I thought was your love for him? If I had suspected that he was in love with Jane Fairfax, I should have warned you accordingly."

"Me!" cried Harriet. "Why should you warn me?—You do not think that I care about Mr. Frank Churchill!"

"I am delighted to hear you speak of him in this way," said Emma, smiling, "but you cannot deny that there was a time—not so very long ago—when you gave me reason to believe that you did care for him?"

"Him!—never, never. Dear Miss Woodhouse, how could you so mistake me?"

"Harriet," cried Emma, after a moment's pause, "what do you mean? Mistake you!—Am I to suppose then——?"

She could not speak another word. Her voice was lost; and she sat down, waiting in great terror for Harriet's answer.

Harriet, who was standing at a little distance, with her face turned away, did not say anything at once. When she spoke, it was in a voice as excited as Emma's.

"Miss Woodhouse, I should not have thought it possible that you could make such a mistake. Mr. Frank Churchill, indeed! No one would ever look at him in the company of—the other. You will remember that we agreed never to name him. When I told you that I should never marry, I knew how immensely he was above me, and I did not dare to hope. But you said that more unlikely things had happened——"

"Harriet," cried Emma, "of whom are you speaking? Let us understand each other now. Are you speaking of—Mr. Knightley?"

"Yes, of course I am. When we talked about him, it was as clear as possible."

"But Harriet; surely we spoke of the great service which Mr. Churchill did for you when he saved you from the gipsies."

"The gipsies! I never thought of the gipsies. No, Miss Woodhouse; but do you remember who danced with me, when I had been so rudely treated by Mr. Elton and his wife? That is something I can never forget."

"And have you any other reason for thinking that he cares about you?"

"Yes," said Harriet, "I have. He was very kind to me at Donwell Abbey. Do you not remember that you came upon us when we were looking across the river at the Abbey-Mill Farm? He spoke to me then in a way which——"

"But, Harriet, you were both looking, as you say, at the Abbey-Mill Farm, and Mr. Knightley knows that Mr. Martin wished to marry you. Do you not think that Mr. Knightley was still thinking of this, and of his hope that you would marry Mr. Martin? I know, indeed, that at one time he did hope that you would."

"No," said Harriet, "I am sure that you are mistaken, Miss Woodhouse. Mr. Martin, indeed! I hope I know better now than to care for Mr. Martin."

With great self-control, Emma made herself say, "Well, Harriet, I will say for Mr. Knightley that he is the last man in the world who, if he could help it, would give any woman the idea that he feels more for her than he really does."

Harriet looked very happy when she heard what her friend said. Emma was saved from further talk upon the subject by the sound of her father's footsteps. Harriet did not wish to meet Mr. Woodhouse and she went out by another door. The moment she was gone, Emma said to herself, "Oh, God! I wish that I had never seen her!"

In the last half hour, as never before, Emma had learned to know her own heart. She said to herself, "Why is it so much worse that Harriet is in love with Mr. Knightley than that she should be in love with Mr. Frank Churchill? Why is the evil so much worse because Harriet has some hope of a return? I know the reason only too well. There is only one person whom George Knightley must marry—and that is, myself!"

Fifty

EMMA AND GEORGE KNIGHTLEY

On the next day, Emma sent a letter to Harriet asking her not to come to Hartfield for a time. "We shall no doubt meet elsewhere, and in the company of others," she wrote, "but I think you will feel, as I do, that for the present we had better not be alone together."

Harriet agreed and was grateful.

One thought was continually in Emma's mind—Mr. Knightley and Harriet Smith! She said to herself, "If Harriet is right in thinking that Mr. Knightley loves her, it will be a far more surprising engagement than that between Frank Churchill and Jane Fairfax. Frank and Jane may be considered equals. But Mr. Knightley and Harriet Smith! Such a rise on her side, and such a fall on his! How it will sink him in the opinion of others! How people will laugh at him behind his back! How sorry John and Isabella will be! Surely, surely it is impossible. Surely Harriet is mistaken in thinking that he loves her and that he means to marry her!"

"And yet"—she went on—"is it impossible? Is it an entirely unknown thing for a gentleman of the highest character to fall in love with a pretty woman who is unworthy of him? Do we not know that such things happen every day? Mr. Knightley—so the Westons tell me—is in London. Perhaps he has gone to tell John and Isabella that he intends to **marry Harriet Smith.**"

Emma decided that if only Harriet's belief that Mr. Knightley loved her could be proved to be mistaken, she would be happy, and would ask for nothing more. "Mr. Knightley and I would then be friends again," she thought, "as we have always been, in spite of the fact that he has so often pointed out my faults to me. He has been a true friend—the best I ever had. And he has always been right, while I so often have been wrong. What terrible mistakes I have made! And now, it seems that I am to be punished for them."

That evening Emma was walking in the garden at Hartfield when she saw the garden door open, and Mr. Knightley walking towards her. She did not know that he had returned from London. She had been thinking of him as sixteen miles away, and she had suddenly to rearrange her thoughts. In half a minute they were together.

"I looked in at the dining-room," he said. "Your father seemed to be asleep, and I thought that I would prefer to be out of doors."

Emma thought that he did not look very happy. "Perhaps," she said to herself, "he has been telling John and Isabella his news about Harriet, and he is pained at the way in which they have received it."

They walked together. He was silent. Emma thought that he was often looking at her, and trying for a fuller view of her face than she wished to give. And this belief produced another fear. Perhaps he wanted to speak to her of his love for Harriet. He might be watching her, hoping that she would say something which would help him to begin. She did not feel that she could help him. He must do it himself. Yet she could not bear this silence. In order to break it, she said, "Now that you are back, you have some news to hear which will surprise you."

"Have I?" he said, quietly. "What kind of news?"

"Oh, of the best possible kind—news of a coming **marriage.**"

"If you mean Frank Churchill and Jane Fairfax, I have heard it already."

"How is it possible?" cried Emma; but then she suddenly thought that he might have stopped at Mrs. Goddard's, and heard the news from Harriet.

"I had a letter on business from Mr. Weston this morning, before I left London, and he added a line to tell me the news."

Emma was glad to know that he had not received the news from Harriet. "You probably felt less surprise than any of us," she said. "You see so much more deeply into these matters than I do." Her voice sank low as she added, "I have made such terrible mistakes."

To her great surprise, she found her arm drawn within his and pressed against his heart.

"Time, my dearest Emma, time alone will heal the wound; time, and your own good sense, and your duty to your father. They will soon be gone, and their home in Yorkshire will be far away. I am sorry, indeed, for Jane Fairfax. She deserves a better fate; and for you, dear Emma, I can only hope that you will soon forget a man who has treated you so badly."

"Mr. Knightley," said Emma, when she had recovered from her surprise, "I must tell you at once that you are mistaken. My blindness to what was going on often led me to act foolishly; and I know now how often I have been wrong, when you could have put me right. But if you think that I was in love with Frank Churchill, you are completely mistaken!"

He was silent for several minutes. Emma's arm was still in his, and as they walked up and down in the failing light, Emma realised that all Harriet's hopes were completely groundless—a mistake, as bad as any of her own. She felt pain and sorrow for Harriet; but she knew the joy in her own heart.

"My dearest Emma," he said at last, "for dearest you will always be to me—whatever answer you give me now. I am not good at making speeches; and my happiness on hearing what you have told me is so great that I scarcely know what I am going to say. If I loved you less, I might be able to talk about it more. But you know what I am. You hear nothing but truth from me. I have blamed you and advised you; and you have borne it as no other woman would have done. But I have loved you, Emma. I have always loved you. Do you think that you can love me a little in return?"

There was a long silence between them. At last Emma began—

"Mr. Knightley—I——"

" 'Mr. Knightley', Emma! I know that, as I once told you, I was sixteen years old when you were born; but must you always call me 'Mr. Knightley'? Will you never call me George?"

"George," she said, softly, and he took her in his arms.

Fifty-one

"POOR MR. WOODHOUSE!"

It was agreed between them that nothing should be said to Mr. Woodhouse for a day or two. Emma and George Knightley both needed time to think about the wonderful change which had happened in their lives, and of its effect upon the lives of others. Emma thought chiefly of her father, and—once more—of poor Harriet.

Emma was very glad to find that Harriet was as anxious as she was that they should not meet. Their letters to one another were painful enough. In order that they might be certain of not meeting for a time, Emma asked Isabella to invite Harriet to London for a few weeks. Harriet wished to pay some visits to a dentist*. There was no dentist in Highbury, and a visit to London was becoming urgent. Isabella at once sent Harriet an invitation, which she accepted. Harriet was taken in Mr. Woodhouse's carriage to Brunswick Square.

* Dentist—a person who repairs and pulls out teeth.

"Emma," said George Knightley, one morning when they were alone together, "I have been thinking of what we are to do. I know that it is impossible for you to leave your father. I have thought that he might perhaps be willing to live with us at Donwell Abbey; but I see now that we cannot ask him to leave Hartfield, and I have thought of another plan. Would your father receive me here at Hartfield? While he lives, I will be a son to him. How happy we could all be together!"

With some difficulty, George Knightley overcame Emma's hesitation about the plan. She had not thought of marrying so soon. Indeed, had she not often said that she would never marry? But at last she agreed, and she talked the matter over with her father.

Poor man!—it was a painful surprise to him. He had suffered so much from people marrying—Isabella, and poor Miss Taylor, and now Emma!

"But, father," said Emma, "this will be very different. Isabella and Miss Taylor went away. I am to stay here. I shall never leave you, and you will have, as well, George Knightley; and you know you have always said that you cannot see him too often. You have been glad to see him every day."

"Well, my dear," said Mr. Woodhouse at last, "you must do as you like—you always do. I am very fond of George Knightley, and of course I shall be glad to have him living here. But all the same, I don't like changes; and I think it a great pity that we cannot all go on as before."

Emma would have been completely happy except for the thought of poor Harriet. She was deeply sorry for Harriet, and she was sorry that there was one secret which she must still hide from George Knightley—the secret of Harriet's love for him.

Harriet was still in London, and the letters of Isabella gave as good an account of her as could be expected.

"At first she seemed unhappy," Isabella wrote, "but we cannot be surprised at this, knowing what she suffers during her visits to the dentist. It appears that more visits will be necessary than was at first expected; but dear Harriet now has more courage. She is happy when she is in the house. She plays with the children, and they are very fond of her. As you know, John and I are hoping to come, with the children, to Hartfield in August. It would give us great pleasure if Harriet would remain with us until then; and, if you agree, she seems glad to do so."

Emma agreed very willingly, and she knew that Harriet would be as well satisfied with the arrangement as she was herself.

"Poor Harriet!" she thought. "No doubt, in time, she will cease to be in love with Mr. Knightley, as she has ceased to be in love with Mr. Elton and with Robert Martin. But this cannot be expected to happen very soon; for Mr. Knightley will do nothing to assist the cure, as Mr. Elton did; he will be very kind to Harriet, but he knows nothing whatsoever of the tender feelings which she has for him. Some day, no doubt, he will be forgotten, and Harriet will fall in love with someone else; but I cannot expect even Harriet to be in love with more than three men in one year."

Emma and Mr. Knightley now decided to allow the news of their engagement to become known in Highbury. Emma first told the Westons, who were made very happy by the news. "It is to be a secret, I suppose," said Mr. Weston. "Such things are always a secret, until it is found that everybody knows about them. Only let me know when I may speak out."

The news spread rapidly, and it was clear that most people were very pleased indeed to hear it; but Mrs. Elton was heard to say, "Poor Knightley! It is a sad business for him. How could he be so taken in? He and Mr. E. were great friends; he would come to dinner whenever he was asked. But now there will be an end of all that. What a silly plan that is of them all living together at Hartfield! It will never do. There was a family near Maple Grove who tried it, and before three months were over, they had to separate."

Fifty-two

HARRIET'S HEART

One morning, when Mr. Knightley came to Hartfield, he said to Emma, "I have something to tell you, Emma; some news."

"Good or bad?" she said, quickly, looking up at him.

"I do not know what it ought to be called."

"Oh, but I see that you are smiling. Surely it must be good news."

"I am very much afraid, my dear Emma, that you will not smile when you hear it."

"Indeed! But why so? I cannot imagine anything which pleases or amuses you which will not please and amuse me too."

"There is one subject," he replied, "and I hope only one, on which we do not think alike." He paused a moment, again smiling, with his eyes fixed upon her face. You will remember what that subject is—Harriet Smith."

She blushed at the name, and she felt afraid of something— she did not know what.

"You must be prepared for the worst," he said—still smiling. "It is bad news for you—Harriet Smith is to marry Robert Martin."

Emma gave a start, and her eyes met his eagerly. They seemed to say, "No, this is impossible!" but her lips were closed.

"It is so, indeed!" continued Mr. Knightley; "I have it from Robert Martin himself. He left me half an hour ago."

Emma was still looking at him in silent surprise

"I knew, my Emma, that you would not like this news," he said. "It is a sad blow for you—and I wish that our opinions were the same. I can only hope that, in time, you will think as I do about Robert Martin."

"You mistake me; you quite mistake me," she cried. "It is not that I am sorry to hear this news, but that I simply cannot believe it! It seems impossible. You cannot mean that Harriet Smith has accepted Mr. Martin. You mean only that he has asked her again."

"I mean exactly what I have said. He has asked her and she has accepted him."

Emma turned her face away in the hope of hiding from him the pleasure and the amusement with which she heard this news.

"Well, now, tell me everything," she said. "Let me know how it happened. I was never more surprised in my life, but the news does not make me unhappy—you are quite mistaken about that."

"It is a very simple story," he replied. "Robert Martin went to London on business three days ago, and I asked him to take some papers for me to John's office. John likes Robert Martin, as I do. On that evening, John and Isabella were taking their two eldest boys and Miss Smith to a circus*. John asked Robert Martin to join them, and Robert could not resist the invitation. They all very much enjoyed the evening, and Robert was asked to dine at Brunswick Square on the next day. He made the most of these two chances of speaking to Miss Smith; and he certainly did not speak unsuccessfully. He returned to Donwell Abbey-Farm this morning a very happy man."

He stopped. Emma did not dare to speak immediately. She was afraid that she would show how happy the news had made her. Her silence made him anxious.

"Emma, my love," he said, "you said that this news would not make you unhappy, but I am afraid that it has done so. You do not think that Robert Martin is good enough for your friend, but I hope that in time you will feel differently about him. He is a friend of mine, and he is a very worthy young man. I am sure that he will be a good husband, although he is not in the rank that you would desire for Miss Smith."

He wanted her to look up and smile; and having now brought herself not to smile too broadly, she said:

* Circus—a show of wild animals and horses.

"You are mistaken about my feelings. I now think that Harriet is very fortunate. I have been silent merely from surprise—extreme surprise; for I have recently had reason to believe that Harriet was even more determined against Mr. Martin than she was before."

"You ought to know your friend best," he replied, "but I should say that she is a good-tempered, soft-hearted girl—not likely to be very determined against any young man who told her that he loved her."

Emma laughed and said, "Well, I am perfectly satisfied, and I sincerely hope that they will be very happy."

"You have changed, indeed," he said, "since the time when you and I first talked about Robert Martin and Harriet Smith."

"I hope so—for at that time I was a fool."

"I have changed also; for I can now see that there is much good in Harriet. You must have noticed that I have tried to know her better. I have talked a good deal with her, and sometimes I was afraid you might think that I was talking about Robert Martin. I never did this; but I came to know her well enough to see how much she has improved under your care."

"My care!" cried Emma. "Ah, poor Harriet!" But she stopped herself, and quietly accepted more praise than she deserved.

Emma felt that she had never been so happy. What more had she to wish for? Nothing, except that she might grow more worthy of the man she loved—the man who had often scolded her, but whose judgment had always been so much better than her own.

She could now look forward with pleasure to Harriet's return; but she felt that she must allow herself to laugh a little at such an end of the sorrowful disappointment of five weeks ago. Such a heart—such a Harriet!

Fifty-three

THREE MARRIAGES

. . AND SO EMMA IS MARRIED . . . .

When the time of sorrow for the death of Mrs. Churchill was over, Frank Churchill and Jane Fairfax were married. They both said how sorry they were that they had deceived so many of their friends, and, in time, their friends forgave them. The mystery of the piano was no longer a mystery. People who were surprised when Frank went to London to get his hair cut could now see that he went there to buy a piano for Jane.

Harriet and Robert Martin were married soon afterwards. Emma was now satisfied that Harriet had given her heart to Robert Martin, and she went to the marriage with great pleasure.

It was now necessary to get Mr. Woodhouse to agree to an early date for the marriage between Emma and George Knightley. When Emma talked to him first about it, he was so unhappy that they were almost hopeless. Emma did not like to see her father suffer; and until he could feel differently she did not feel that she could go on with the marriage. But slowly he became used to the idea and at last he agreed that the date for it should be fixed. He perhaps agreed more easily because a thief was active in Highbury at this time, and he thought that when Mr. Knightley lived at Hartfield the thief would be less likely to come there.

The wedding was very much like the other weddings where those who are to be married have no wish for fine clothes and a grand show. Mrs. Elton said, "The dresses were very poor; not nearly so good as when I was married. It was all a very poor show. I quite pitied them." But, in spite of this, the hopes and good wishes of the small band of true friends who were in the church were fulfilled in the perfect happiness of the pair.

LIST OF EXTRA WORDS